THE BAILEY BROTHERS

BAILEY CLAN WESTERNS
BOOK TWO

TERENCE NEWNES

CHAPTER 1

THE TOWN OF RED
BUTTE

THEY RODE INTO THE TOWN OF RED BUTTE IN NEW Mexico Territory. Two tall and lean young men, covered in trail dust, for they had ridden far, and all they wanted was a drink to wash away the taste of the dust and a meal that they had not cooked for themselves. They swung down from their saddles before the Bison Head saloon, and tying their horses to the hitching rail, they banged the dust off their clothes with their hats and then walked into the bar. The two young men were brothers, Brian and Mark Bailey. Both had chiseled features with a strong chin and grey-blue eyes, and it was easy to see that they were related. Brian was a Civil War veteran and the elder of the two at twenty-seven, while Mark was twenty-five. They were on their way to Arizona, hoping to make money from the goldfields so that they could start a ranch of their own. Starting a good-sized ranch needed money, and they were hoping to make that in the goldfields.

They walked up to the bar and Brian told the barkeep, a balding middle-aged man with a limp who looked like a retired puncher, "Whiskey for two, and make them doubles." The

1

barkeep poured their drinks, and Brian asked him, "Friend, could you point us to the best eating place in town? We've been on the trail for a long time, eating our own cooking, and we're sure looking forward to some good food!" The barkeep gave him a long look and then said, "The Beef Steak, just down the street, is the best." He hesitated and then asked, "You boys just passing through, or are you looking for work here?" Brian smiled at him and said, "Friend, just as soon as we finish our drink here, we're going to the Beef Steak for a good meal, and then we'll be on our way." Mark commented, "Yeah, we want no part in whatever's going down in this town right now." The barkeep gave them a speculative look and then moved away.

Both the brothers had scanned the room as soon as they had entered, and they could sense the tension in the place. They had no doubt that trouble was building, but Mark was sincere when he said that they wanted no part of whatever was going on in the town. They were both young in years but battle-hardened veterans of trouble, and they could size up a situation in a glance. At the hitching rail, they had noted two horses wearing the Box T brand and five horses wearing the Double B brand. There were quite a few men in the saloon, but at the bar stood five men together, and at a table sat a blond-haired youngster who looked barely eighteen years old, talking to a tough-looking cowboy who must have been over thirty. The five men at the bar kept glancing at the two punchers at the table. Brian and Mark just needed the one look at the five to peg them as gunmen for hire; they had seen a few in their time. They downed their drinks and were turning to leave when one of the five men said, "Hold it there! Just stay where you are!" Two of the men had moved across to the side of the room while one had moved to stand by the door. The man still standing at the bar, who had just spoken, was a broad-faced, clean-shaven man of average height who wore two tied-down guns and whose attention was now directed at the two men sitting at the table. The last man was moving slowly towards the table where the two cowboys sat. It was obvious to the brothers that the five men were boxing in the two cowboys.

The man moving towards the table, a tall broad-shouldered man with a low-slung tied-down gun, had approached from the side so that he was facing both the cowboys, who looked up at his approach. The older, tough-looking cowboy started to get up, but the man said, "Sit still! You're covered from all sides. There's one man at the door and two behind you, so make a move and you're dead!" The youngster said, "So you're with the Double B? I ain't seen you around before." The tall man told him with a grim smile, "And you won't see me after this either. Both of you stand up slowly and unbuckle your gun belts. Make a wrong move and we'll shoot you where you stand." Both the cowboys stood up slowly, and the blond-haired youngster said, "Even if we drop our gun belts, you're going to shoot us anyway!" The tall man shrugged and told him, "You can die here or outside on the street, your choice!"

Suddenly, a voice from the bar spoke loud and clear, "I never did like to see a fixed fight." It was Mark who had spoken, and Brian sighed and told the man at the bar with the two tied-down guns, "Don't try it, Mister! Not if you want to stay healthy." The man had shifted his attention to Mark when he spoke up, and his hand was sweeping down for his gun when Brian warned him. His hand was on his gun butt, but he froze when he found himself staring at the gun in Brian's hand. The other four men had also turned at Mark's voice, and they saw the gun in Mark's hand. That distraction was enough for the cowboys, and the youngster and the tough-looking cowboy had drawn their guns as well. Brian gestured with his gun and told the man at the bar, "Go over there and join those two." The man stared at him in anger, and Brian said mildly, "Or I could just shoot you in the knee, your choice!" The man glared at him for a moment longer but then turned and went to join the two who were standing at the side of the room. Mark told the tall man at the table and the one standing by the door, "You two move over there as well. I maybe ought to tell you not to make any sudden moves, but what the hell, if you feel lucky you just go right ahead." The tall man said angrily, "There are still five of us, and we still have our guns! It looks to me like it's you two who are gonna need some luck!"

Two shots rang out, and the two men who had first moved to the side of the room stared stupidly at their right hands dripping blood. One was shot in the forearm, and one in the biceps. Brian said in a mild voice, "That's true, what you just said, but we don't believe in luck, so now there are three of you." The tall man stared at the smoking gun in Brian's fist, and he slowly licked his lips. The stocky, broad-faced man who had first told the brothers to stay put, now snarled at Brian, "You're a big man when you got the drop! Leather it, and we'll see just how fast you are!" It was Mark who answered him. "Mister," he told him, "your first mistake was to stop us from leaving this here bar, and now your second mistake is to challenge us to a gunfight. Move to the center of the room!" He then told the tall man, "You join your sidekicks over there at the side of the room." The tall man walked across the room, and the stocky gunman moved to the center and faced Brian.

The blond-haired youngster had been staring in fascination at the brothers and at what was happening, and now he said, "I don't know who you gentlemen are, but I'm mighty glad you're here. We got those four covered, so you just forget about them!" Brian faced the stocky gunman and slid his gun into his holster. The gunman snarled, "Now you..." His hand was streaking for his gun as he spoke, and then a shot rang out, and he fell dead with a hole in the middle of his forehead. Mark said conversationally, "You could have at least waited until he had completed what he was going to say." Brian shrugged and replied, "Well, as Dad always says…" Mark interrupted him, "Yeah, yeah, I know. If you're going to shoot, don't wait for the sun to set. Seems like nobody gave such good advice to that hombre; he just couldn't stop talking!" Brian told the remaining four gunmen, "Drop your gun belts and you can leave. But do it now before I change my mind!" There was no hesitation or talk; the men dropped their gun belts and left the saloon.

The blond-haired youngster and the older cowboy came over, and the barkeep told the brothers, "I thought you boys said that you didn't want to get involved in whatever was happening in this here town!" Mark shrugged and told him, "And we didn't! We were just about to leave when that gent lying dead there ordered us not to leave." Brian said, "We couldn't just stand here and let them carry out their ambush. Bushwhackers are our least favorite people!" The blond youngster came up to them and said, "Boy! Am I ever grateful that you two stepped in, or we'd be dead by now!" He stuck out his hand and said, "I'm Rick Taylor of the Box T, and this here is our Segundo, Trent Williams." They all shook hands, and Brian said, "I'm Brian Bailey, and this man here who just can't keep his nose out of trouble is my brother, Mark." Trent Williams sighed and gestured to the dead man, "These must be new hires of the Double B, which was why they caught us off guard. We're going to have to be mighty careful and suspicious of every stranger in future!" Brian laughed, and Trent said with a wry smile, "Present company excepted!" Mark interrupted and said, "It was nice meeting you gentlemen, but my stomach is starting to think that my brain has died, so if you don't mind, we'll just mosey on down to that Beef Steak place and have us some good food." Rick said eagerly, "Mind if we join you? Least I can do is buy you a good steak, and the Beef Steak has the best in the country!"

They walked into the Beef Steak eating house and were

surprised to find that the place was clean and neat. They sat down, and a buxom lady came over to their table. "Hi Rick, Trent!" she said. "Was that gunfire I just heard? You boys shooting some more Double B gunmen?" Rick laughed and introduced the brothers, saying, "Brian, Mark, this lady is Pam McGowan, and she owns this place. She also makes the best food in the country! Pam, these here are the Bailey brothers." Brian and Mark stood up and shook hands with Pam, and Mark said, "Pleased to meet you, Ma'am. I'm hungry as a lobo wolf, and I'll take two of everything you've got!" They were served thick, juicy steaks with roast gravy for the fresh bread and four eggs each with bacon on the side. No one spoke as they ate, and it was obvious that the brothers were hungry and had healthy appetites. Finally they sat back with a contented sigh, and Brian told Pam, "Ma'am, I ain't seen eggs in a coon's age, and that steak must have been made in heaven!" She laughed and said, "Call me Pam; everyone here does." Mark said, "Well, Pam, I might just stick around for a while just to eat your cooking every day!" She laughed again, but her eyes were curious, and she said, "So you're not with the Box T?"

It was Rick who answered, "They are just passing through, but they pulled us out of a very tight corner at the Bison Head. There were five new gunmen of the Double B that we hadn't seen before, and they had us boxed in and were getting ready to plant us on Boot Hill when Mark and Brian here took a hand in the game." Pam looked the brothers over and told Rick in a serious tone, "Were I you, I would try to stop them from passing through." She looked at Brian and explained, "I know Jack Donovan; he's eaten here before. My husband was in his unit during the war, and he died on one of their raids. We've all heard of the Cedar Creek battle!" Rick stared at Mark and exclaimed, "My God! You are *those* Baileys? No wonder those five didn't stand a chance!" He turned to Pam and said, "Brian drew on one of those gunmen, and I've never seen a faster draw!" Brian looked uncomfortable and said, "Kid, Mark is much faster than I am. Besides, no one is faster than Jack Donovan!" Rick asked him, "But will you stay and help us out? Truth be told, we need all the help we can get now that Bart Baker is still hiring gunmen!" But it was Mark who told him, "Anyway, tell us about the trouble here. Why is this Baker hiring so many gunmen, and why does he want to kill you?" So Rick told him how the fight between the two ranches began.

Ruth and Harry Taylor owned the Box T, and they had one daughter named Sally aged 16 and one son Rick aged 18. They had started the Box T around 10 years ago, and Harry, being a savvy rancher, had made it pay. Bart Baker had come in with a large herd and had started the Double B five years ago. The Box T was half the size of the Double B in rangeland, but much better managed by Harry Taylor. He actually legally owned all the range that he claimed for the Box T. He had chosen well, and the Box T range had good sources of water, with the Red Butte creek running through it. Harry Taylor never overstocked his range, and he had dug wells and built check dams to hold water for the dry season, so his stock were always well fed and did not have to lose weight by walking miles to get to water in the dry season.

Bart Baker legally owned just two claims that he had filed on, and the rest of his range he just claimed as his own, which was the custom of big ranchers in those days. But unlike Harry Taylor, Bart Baker was not a savvy rancher, and he mostly left the running of the ranch to his foreman Len Spalding, who unfortunately was more a gunman than a rancher himself. The Double B had two streams running through their range, and the water would have been sufficient if they had not overstocked their range. But Baker wanted to be called the king of the range, and he always strode hard-booted on the boardwalks whenever he came to town. He had money, and he bought more cattle and overstocked his range, which was okay during the wet spell. But when the dry spell hit, then the water from the streams could not sustain such large herds and started to dry up. He was lucky during the first four years as the dry spells did not last long and so his cattle survived. But neither he nor his foreman learnt any lessons, and they did not build catchments to hold the runoff rainwater, nor did they dig wells like Harry Taylor had done.

During the fourth year of the existence of the Double B, there was an extremely long dry spell, and the two streams started to dry up and the cattle began dying of thirst. Baker met Harry Taylor in town and demanded that the Double B cattle be allowed to drink from the Red Butte creek. He did not ask, he demanded, but still Harry told him, "I would if I could; I hate to see them cattle dying like that. But no range can hold such a vast herd with the water that is available here. If I allowed your cattle on my range, then my water would also dry up, and I would end up like you; with *my* cattle dying as well. My advice to you would be to sell most of your cattle right now for whatever you can get." Baker shouted at him, "I didn't ask for your advice! I'm going to drive my cattle to the creek, and I'd like to see you stop me!" Harry said mildly, "Oh, I'll stop you, but I would advise you not to try that." The mouth of the Red Butte creek was towards the end of the Box T range and just about two miles from the boundary line of the property, which abutted the land claimed by the Double B. Harry Taylor was a mild-mannered man who did not stride hard-booted on the board-walks, and so Bart Baker took him to be a man without courage; but he was soon to learn differently.

The Box T had a crew of eleven riders, plus the foreman Trent Williams; together with Harry and his son Rick, that made up a crew of fourteen. After the threat made by Baker, Harry took steps to safeguard the Box T. A week after Baker had made the threat, he carried it out. His men drove a large herd of over five hundred head across the boundary line, headed for Red Butte creek. When the herd had covered a mile of Box T land, two men of the Box T with rifles began firing on the front line of the cattle. The men were in well-fortified sites and had plenty of ammunition. They dropped a dozen head of cattle, but the riders of the Double B kept driving the cattle forward. From another well-protected lookout point, Harry Taylor and Rick watched what was happening, and Harry sighed and said to his son, "I hate to see cattle die like this, but we have no choice. This is a matter of our survival!" He and Rick struck matches and set fire to fuse wires that were placed near them, and about a minute later, almost simultaneous explosions blew the herd apart and some of the Double B riders as well. Harry had previously carefully sited and placed buried dynamite, and the fuses led to the place where father and son were making their stand. It was later estimated that around a hundred head of cattle died that day before the rest turned and stampeded back to the Double B. Three of their hands died in the explosions, and another five were trampled to death by the stampeding herd. It was after that shock that Baker started bringing in gunmen. He now claimed that the mouth of Red Butte creek was on his range and therefore belonged to him. Unfortunately for him, Harry proved that he legally owned all the land that he claimed.

"So now Baker has sworn that he would take that part of the range, even if he has to kill us all to do it," Rick concluded. "We've been careful," said Trent. "None of our boys move anywhere alone, and we have signals to alert the rest of the crew. One shot means that danger is coming soon, two means that the danger is close, and three shots mean that there is a fight taking place." Brian asked him, "So how many guns has he hired so far?" Trent said, "He had about seven of the original crew remaining after the explosions which includes his foreman, Len Spalding. Then he brought in about ten hired guns and they tried to raid the Box T. But we had prepared fortified shooting sites at strategic places, and the hired guns ran into a hail of lead, which left about four of them dead." Rick took up the tale again and said, "The remaining gunmen started hanging out in town, laying in wait for us to come in. But as Trent here just explained, our boys don't travel alone, and three more gunmen died here in town."

Trent then continued and said, "The trouble is that four of our men are wounded and out of action, which leaves us with just ten, and that includes Harry and Rick here. Now it seems that Baker is hiring more men, judging by what happened at the Bison Head today." Brian asked him, "Where does the barkeep stand in all this? I ask because I saw his hand go under the bar when the trouble began, and I guess he has a shotgun or rifle there for trouble." Rick laughed and told him, "That's ole Pat Fields! He used to ride for us until a steer fell on his leg, and my dad helped him start the Bison Head saloon. He would have taken a hand in the game, but with five of them spread out, we would have wound up dead anyway. You drawing cards in the game was what saved us." Brian said, "You seem to be having things under control, so I don't think you would need us. Anyway, we're on our way to Arizona, to the goldfields, to make us a stake to start our own ranch." Pam, who had sat in on the discussion, now told Brian, "The reason Rick and Trent came to town today was because I sent for them. Yesterday I came to know that Len Spalding has hired the Boynton brothers, and he expects them to get here any day now."

Trent interrupted, "They are Utah gunmen, and they have a bad reputation. It's been said that they are borderline outlaws who have always managed to escape the law. Blaze and Red Boynton always work together, and they are known as the fastest guns in Utah." Pam continued speaking and said, "That's not all, because he's also sent for Dave Schwartz, the Nevada gunman." Trent told Brian, "They do say that there's no one faster than Dave Schwartz, or Black Dave as he's called. He's said to have killed at least ten men in stand-up shootouts. Black Dave will always face his opponent, and you'll get a fair shake from him, but the Boynton boys never give anyone a fair shake. While you're facing one of them in a shootout, the other will shoot you from cover! Rumor has it that they're not above bushwhacking a target if they feel that's the best way to get the job done. They are just killers for hire, and it's been said that they don't give a damn who the target is; man, woman, or child as long as the money is good."

Mark asked them, "Who's the town Marshal and where does he stand in this fight?" Pam shook her head and said, "Paul Lee is over fifty and has a game leg, so he can't do long hours in the saddle. That's why he got the job of town Marshal. He's a good man and well liked, and he'll fight to keep the town safe, but what happens on the range is not his job, and as I said, he can't do long hours in the saddle anyway." Mark looked at Brian and said, "Maybe we could just stay over for a couple of days or a week. Sort of get some rest before the long ride to the goldmines?" Brian looked at his brother, and then he looked at Rick's golden hair. He smiled at Mark and said, "You're thinking of Bruce!" When Pam looked a question, Brian explained, "Bruce McCullough of the Double M. He married our sister Betsy, and he has golden hair like Rick. I guess that's why Mark decided to butt in at the Bison Head!" Mark asked again, "So can we stay put for a week?"

Brian thought about it for a moment and then asked Pam, "Do you think the town Marshal would hire two deputies who would work for just food and board?" Pam's eyes opened wide, and then she laughed and told him, "Of course he will, and be glad to get you two! Your food and board is on me. I have some rooms upstairs that I sometimes rent out, and you can use that to hang your hats." Brian smiled and said, "Your food decided me on staying!" Turning to Rick, he "First thing tomorrow morning, we will need to scout your range and the surrounding areas between your ranch and the town to get an idea of the layout. We would also need to see where the

Double B is and what trails lead into this part of the country."
Trent said that he would come in the next day and take the
brothers for a ride across the country. Brian and Mark retired
to their rooms, and tired as they were, they fell asleep as soon
as they lay down.

The next morning, after a good and heavy breakfast, Pam
took them over to the Marshal's office. Paul Lee stood up and
came out from behind his desk as soon as they walked in.
"Morning, Pam," he said. "I take it these are the two young men
who sent the Double B gunmen packing last night?" Pam
nodded and introduced them. Paul Lee was a well-built man
who walked with a pronounced limp, favoring his right leg. He
had a craggy face with deep-set eyes and hair that was almost
fully grey. Brian started to explain what had happened in the
Bison Head, but the Marshal cut him off. "No need for explana-
tions," he said. "I have my lookouts in town who let me know
when trouble is brewing. I was just about to leave this office for
the Bison Head, when I heard the shooting and a man told me
that it was all over." He grimaced and said, "This bum leg of
mine makes it difficult for me to move fast at any time, so I'm
grateful that you boys took a hand and saved Rick Taylor." Brian
pointed to the leg and asked him, "What happened? If you don't
mind my asking."

The Marshal shrugged and told him, "About five years ago,
my horse stepped in a gopher hole and I was a bit late in
jumping clear. The horse landed on my leg, and I was trapped.
The leg was broke and I couldn't get free, so I shot the horse to
put it out of its misery, and I spent the night just lying there. It
was late the next morning that I was found by some Box T
hands, by which time I was unconscious and almost dead; or so
they told me later. The doc tried his best, but he said that the
bone would never knit fully, mainly because he didn't get to set
it in time." Pam said, "Paul had a small farm at the edge of the
Box T range, but after the accident he gave it up and became

Marshal instead." Turning to Paul, she said, "Brian and Mark here would like to be your deputies without pay."

The Marshal was curious and asked Brian, "Why not just sign on with the Box T?" But Brian explained, "We did not want to get involved in this here range war, but now we are, and so we would like to help by enforcing the law impartially since we really don't know either of the warring factions." He paused to gather his thoughts and then continued, "We are actually on our way to the goldmines for a stake to start our own ranch, and once this trouble is over, that's where we'll be headed. I guess the only reason we are involved is because Rick reminded Mark here of our brother-in-law, Bruce. He's also young with golden hair!" Paul Lee smiled and said, "Well, boys, whatever the reason may be, I'm mighty glad to have you as my deputies." He went to the desk and came back with two badges, which he pinned on them and duly swore them in as Deputy Town Marshals.

After pinning on the badge, Brian asked him, "Marshal, I'm just curious. I know Pam has recommended us, but how do you know if we are capable of doing the job?" The Marshal seemed to contemplate that question for a long moment and then said, "Way back about 12 years or so, there was a range war in Kansas, and a family that had started a small farm was dragged into it. One of the sons, a young lad of 14, ended that war in a shootout. I was one of the small farmers there at the time, and the drought ended my farm as well, but I never forgot that family. There was no backup to them. Like the rest of us small farmers there, that family also stayed neutral during the fighting, but when they were dragged into it, they just went about ending it." He looked at Brian and said, "I think you were that young lad!" Brian shrugged and said, "Yes, that's true. Mark here was just 12 at the time, but he was a man grown with that rifle in his hands!" The Marshal told them, "Your idea is a good one. Lay down the law impartially and enforce it. Harry has already proved to Baker, right here in this office, that he legally owns that range, so for Baker to now try and take it by force puts him outside the law. Now that you know how she stands, you go ahead and do whatever you need to. When you need me, I'll be here, and I'll back you up in town; but riding the range is something that I just can't do anymore." Trent Williams then came in and took Brian and Mark for a ride around the country.

CHAPTER 2
THE BAILEYS

BRIAN AND MARK BAILEY WERE ORIGINALLY FROM THE Tennessee hills. Their father, Nolan Bailey, came from the feuding Bailey clan, which had a long-running feud with the Hawkes clan. But when Nolan turned seventeen, he met and fell in love with Kate Hawkes. They tried their best to keep their love a secret because they knew that their families would never agree to it. But love cannot be hidden for long, and one day two of Kate's cousins braced Nolan in the hills. He shot and killed both of them, but they got two bullets into him before they died. It took him a month to recover from his wounds, and then he and Kate went down to the flatlands and found a preacher to marry them. Strangely enough, after their marriage, the feud between the families died down; and while they never became friends, at least they stopped killing each other.

Nolan and Kate had five children: Mike, Brian, Mark, Luke, and Betsy. They had struggled to raise their five children on their small farm in Tennessee, and Nolan used to go west for months at a time to trap for furs and hunt buffalo for the hides. So when their eldest son Mike turned sixteen, the entire family migrated westwards. They first settled on a farm in Kansas, but two years of drought left them with nothing, and they moved to Colorado. All the children were taught at an early age to handle firearms, and they were all expert sharpshooters with a rifle. Brian was faster in drawing his pistol than Mike and accurate in his shooting, but it was Mark who later became the fastest gun in the family. However, the family's first choice of weapon was always the rifle, and they were all experts in its use.

In Kansas, the family had stayed neutral in a war between two big ranches, the Bar T and the Rocking R, until gunmen from the Rocking R insulted Kate in town and then tried to draw against Mike and died in the trying. Nolan and his two sons, Mike and Brian, finally ended the war by destroying the fighting force of the Rocking R. Brian was just fourteen at the time. In Colorado, they started to prosper when they took to raising cattle, but rustlers and an extremely cold winter wiped them out. Mike and Brian had taken out after the rustlers, and in a shootout, they killed four of them, but they could not shoot their way out of the worst winter in many years that hit Colorado. They were broke, with no money to restock their ranch, and so they left Colorado and moved to Gila City to mine gold and raise a stake for their future. They worked hard during the gold rush and got together a nice stake to start their own ranch. They had heard of the cattle ranches in Texas, and so the decision was made to settle in Texas and start ranching in a big way, which they did. But on the way to Texas, Kate was killed during an Indian attack, and so they named their ranch in Texas the Rafter K, in honor of Kate.

In Texas, they joined forces with their neighbor, the Double M ranch owned by Ryan and Maria McCullough, in a war with a carpetbagger who tried to take over their ranches. They won the war, and Ryan's son Bruce married Betsy Bailey. Everything was peaceful after the war with the carpetbagger, but two years later, Brian and Mark decided to leave home in search of a stake to start their own ranch, which was how they stumbled into the range war in Red Butte.

Brian and Mark studied the terrain they were riding through as they rode from the town to the Box T. There was good grassland for cattle, and there were mesas in the distance, but near the town was a large red sandstone butte for which the town was named. It was a rolling land, and here and there the trail went through arroyos, and they studied the slopes with care. The brothers made a note of all the places where an ambush could easily take place and places where a man might fort up for a fight. It wasn't as though either of them expected an ambush or was looking to find a place where they might make a stand if attacked; it was just what they did naturally, without thinking about it, wherever they went. In this wide-open, wild land, a man never knew when he might pass that way again, and then, if trouble was chasing him, knowledge of the terrain was always important. That was the way of most seasoned travelers in the West at that time, and the brothers were very seasoned travelers.

They arrived at the Box T ranch house and were met at the front door by Rick. He took them inside and introduced them to his parents and sister. Harry Taylor was a tall, good-looking man in his early forties with dark hair, thin angular features, and cool grey eyes. His wife Ruth was a good-looking blonde lady about five years younger than her husband. Their daughter Sally had inherited her mother's good looks, and both she and her brother Rick had their mother's blonde hair. Sally was just sixteen, but for that time in the West she was a woman grown, and many girls her age were usually married. Harry told the brothers, "Rick told me about what happened last night in town, and we are in your debt for saving his life." The brothers looked uncomfortable, and Brian changed the topic by saying, "We are now deputy town Marshals and we came here to look over the range, especially the creek that Baker claims. Then we are going to ride over to the Double B and have a talk with Baker to see if we can't bring an end to this fight." Harry shook his head and said, "Good luck with that! Baker wants to be king of the range, and he just won't listen to reason." Brian started to say something, but Harry held up his hand to stop him. "I know it's something you have to do, and I understand that," he said. "I'm just telling you how the man is so that you'll know what to expect. He could even order his men to attack you if he thinks you're trying to take my side!"

Mark looked thoughtful and asked Harry, "You mean he would actually shoot down a lawman?" Harry shrugged and said, "The men who waited in town for us to come in told one of our boys, before they shot it out, that they were told to gun down the Marshal if he interfered." Brian said, "Well, it's still our duty to go over and try to talk some sense into the man. After that, we'll play it whichever way he wants; but as a lawman, it's my duty to talk first." Trent Williams was listening to the conversation, and now he asked Brian, "And if you were not a lawman?" It was Mark who answered him. "If someone is out to get us," he said with a shrug, "we don't usually waste our time trying to change his mind. We figure a man looking for trouble should find it, so we save him the time of searching." Brian smiled at the Taylors and said, "Don't mind him; he isn't as bloodthirsty as he sounds." Turning to Mark, he said, "But now we *are* lawmen, so let's go do some law work!"

They rode to the boundary line, and Trent Williams pointed out the Red Butte creek. Further on, they saw the craters in the ground where the explosions had taken place, and then Trent Williams pointed out the boundary markers to them and told them how to get to the Double B ranch house. Brian and Mark rode on with their rifles in their hands, and they kept a sharp lookout all around as they rode. They saw a lot of cattle along the way, and they noted that the cattle were mostly thin with their bones protruding. The grass on the range was scanty, and they figured that the cattle had eaten the grass right down to the roots, which wasn't good for any cattle ranch. They passed a stream that had just a trickle of muddy water flowing.

They reached the ranch house, and they were challenged by two men who seemed to be standing guard. Brian pointed to his badge and said, "Deputy Marshals from the town. We're here to talk to Bart Baker." He paused and added, "Peacefully! Just to talk!" One of the men said, "Wait here!" He told the other man to stay put, and he went up to the ranch house. After a moment, he came out and waved them in. They tied their horses to the hitching rail and walked up to the house, still holding their rifles. The guard ushered them in and they came face to face with a tall, broad-shouldered, tough-looking man in his late forties. He had a thin face with an aquiline nose, and his scanty hair was receding from his forehead. As Mark would later describe him, "His face had a permanent sour expression, and when he spoke, it was obvious that he had a permanent sour disposition as well!" Now he looked at the brothers and said, "Well? I never heard of Paul Lee having any deputies!" Brian said mildly, "That's because he deputized us just this morning." Bart looked at them closely and said, "You two seem to match the description my men gave of the two drifters who attacked them in town last night!" Mark shrugged and told him, "Actually, they were trying to kill two cowboys after boxing them in, and we just told them to stop." Baker snarled, "So how did one of them die and two of them get wounded?" Brian still spoke mildly and said, "Well, we told them, but they didn't listen." Before Baker could say anything more, he continued, "But we came here to ask you officially to end this war. We've seen the deeds that the Box T has, and it proves beyond doubt that the range they claim is theirs legally, so you cannot claim the Red Butte creek as yours."

Baker shouted, "Get out of here! You may be a Marshal in the town, but out here you have no authority. I'll take that land and no one is going to stop me!" Brian said, "Whoever is running this ranch has no idea about the cattle business. We've seen enough on our way here to know that much. My advice would be to talk to Harry Taylor as a neighbor and get him to help you in running this place properly." Baker became red in the face and he almost screamed, "Get out! I told you, over here you don't have any authority, and that tin badge means nothing." Brian sighed and told him, "We carry our own authority in our hands. Since you refuse to listen to reason, we are going to have to take you to town so that the Marshal can talk to you." Before the blustering Baker could say anything, Brian lifted his rifle barrel slightly so that it pointed at his stomach and said, "I would be much obliged if you would lead the way to our horses and also lead the way to town. See, we are new here, and we might get lost, so you can show us the way to town." Bart Baker stared at their rifles and then stared at them, and what he saw in their faces made the anger run out of him like water down a steep hillside. He was a headstrong and arrogant man, but he was no fool where men were concerned. He knew these were dangerous men and that they wouldn't hesitate to shoot him if they were threatened by his men.

He walked out and called to one of the guards, "Get me my horse; I'm going with these men to town. Where's Len?" The guard shouted out, and Len Spalding came out of the bunkhouse. "Saddle up," Baker told him. "You're coming to town with me." He turned to Brian and said grimly, "If that's all right with you!" Brian shrugged and said, "No problem. Both of you can show us the way to town. That way we sure won't get lost!" They rode to town with Baker and Len in front, and the brothers followed with their rifles across their saddlebows. When they reached the outskirts of the town, Baker said, "Well, you got here safely, so we'll ride back now." But Brian told him,

"I'm serious, and I'm being impartial when I tell you to end this war and talk to the Box T like a good neighbor. That Harry Taylor knows cattle and range management, and I'm sure that he will be willing to help you out." For a moment, Baker seemed to hesitate, but then Len Spalding snarled, "I don't need that bum to advise me on how to run a ranch! We've just had bad luck with these long dry spells, and he should have been willing to share that water."

Mark looked at him for a long moment and then said, "You know, it's funny how these long dry spells haven't hurt the Box T as much as they have the Double B!" Len Spalding glared at him and was about to retort when Baker swung his horse around to leave and told them, "I've said what my stand is, that range is mine and I'll take it. You boys better look at your hole card before deciding to stay in this game. There's bad weather coming!" He rode away without waiting for an answer, and Len Spalding followed him. Brian sighed as they rode into town and said, "Well, we tried to talk sense into him." They reined in before the Marshal's office, and Brian said, "Mark, you take a look around town and be careful, you hear? I'll talk to the Marshal and then join you." Mark raised his hand and said, "Sure, boss!" Then he laughed and rode to the Bison Head while Brian hitched his horse to the rail and walked into the Marshal's office.

Paul Lee asked him, "So how did it go?" Brian told him everything and then said, "At the last there, when I spoke to Baker at the town limits, he seemed to hesitate, as though he partly agreed with what I was saying. But then Len Spalding shot off his mouth and Baker's arrogance took over, and he warned us and rode away." Paul had a curious look on his face and asked Brian, "But why bring Baker to the town limits in the first place? You obviously didn't bring him in to talk to me." Brian grinned and told him, "I said he had to lead the way to town as we were new and we might get lost. I guess I sort of accidentally tilted my rifle barrel to point at his stomach as I spoke." Paul Lee laughed out loud, "I'm getting dumb in my old age! That was a smart move! I told you I knew you could handle this job." Turning serious, he said, "That day when your father and your brother and you went to the Rocking R, a few of us small farmers were up on the hill some distance away. We had heard about the order to shoot your family on sight, and we knew you would go to the Rocking R, so we went there to back you up." He was silent for a while as though remembering that day, and then he continued, "As it turned out, we weren't needed at all. But I still remember that young lad standing there facing Ray Rayburn." He looked up at Brian and said, "It wasn't the fact that you were fast on the draw that impressed me. What impressed me was that you had faith in your father's judgment, and you faced Rayburn without fear!" He shook his head and said, "And you were all of fourteen years old!" Brian again looked uncomfortable as he didn't like to listen to anyone praising him. He stood up and said, "I better go see what young Mark is up to. That boy just loves trouble!" Paul Lee smiled to himself as Brian left, for he knew these real tough men were uncomfortable with praise or thanks.

Brian found Mark at the Beef Steak, talking to Pam McGowan. As soon as he entered, she said, "You boys sit down and I'll bring you something to eat." She sat down with them as they ate and asked Brian, "Mark told me about what happened with Baker, so what now?" Brian pondered the question as he ate. "I'm reminded of what Jack said when he became a lawman for a while in Abilene, Kansas," he finally said. "He said that he would do the job his way, and he did. I think that now that we have done our duty in talking to Baker, it's time to do this our way." Pam looked quizzical, and Mark explained, "Our way is to take the fight to the enemy. We don't believe in waiting for them to choose the time or the place." Pam asked Brian, "So what exactly will you do? The Box T will back you up, but as you know, they are just loyal ranch hands who ride for the brand. But you know all that, and you know that they can't stack up to the likes of the Boyntons or Black Dave. So that just leaves you two, and I'm worried because I think that I'm responsible for getting you involved in this fight." Brian shrugged and told her, "If anyone got us involved in this fight, it was Mark here, so don't you go blaming yourself!" Mark told her, "I'll tell you what his plan is because I know how he thinks. He's going to wait for the Boyntons and Black Dave to get here, and then we're going to face them and call them out. Then we'll take the Box T and we'll go to the Double B and end this war." Pam was still worried and said, "The Boyntons don't believe in a fair fight. Maybe you should just take the Box T and go to the Double B right now and end this!" Brian said, "We are still lawmen at the moment, and while we intend to end this fight our way, we still have to wait for Baker to actually bring in the gunmen. Once that happens, then his plans are in the open, and we will be free to act, so we just have to wait."

They took a turn around the town and inspected all the saloons and stores, and told everyone that when anyone spotted any strangers in town, they were to immediately inform the Marshal or his deputies. Their final stop was at the Bison Head saloon, and Pat Fields poured them a drink. "Heard you boys have been mighty busy," he said. He pointed at the badges and said, "You boys have a funny way of avoiding trouble!" Mark laughed and told him, "Our Pa always says that the best way to avoid trouble is to face it head on!" Pat shook his head slowly and said, "That's original! Anyway, I'm mighty glad you showed up when you did. The Box T was my home, and as far as I'm concerned, I still ride for the brand!" Suddenly he looked over at the door and said in a low voice, "Two strangers are walking in right now." Brian and Mark casually turned around and looked at the newcomers. One was tall and one was short, and both looked dirty and unkempt, but Brian noted that their guns looked clean and well cared for. The taller man had a thin face with high cheekbones and small, shifty eyes. The smaller man looked like a weasel with dirty red hair but had a thickset body. They came up to the bar, and the taller man told Pat, "Whiskey! And maybe you can tell us if anyone from the Double B ranch is around town." The smaller man looked at Brian and Mark, and noting the badges, he said, "Marshal, maybe you could direct us to the Double B." Brian gave him a cool look and then told Mark, "Go see if anyone from the Double B is around."

Mark walked to the door, and Brian told the smaller man, "I take it that you're the Boynton brothers. You must be Red." He told the taller man, who had turned halfway around to face him, "Which makes *you* Blaze Boynton." There was a sudden cautious look on Blaze Boynton's face, and he said, "Yeah, that's true, Marshal. We were hired by the Double B, and we're here to join up." Brian made a disgusted face and said, "You mean you're here to do some killing! Now, both of you can drop your gun belts and ride out of here, or you can try your luck in a fair fight. Either way, you're not joining the Double B!" The Boyntons slowly moved apart and faced Brian with their hands hovering over their guns. "You think you can take us both, Marshal?" Blaze asked him. Brian shrugged and told him, "I think I can, but that man at the door insists on making it a fair fight, two against two!" The Boyntons froze and slowly looked at the door to see Mark standing there with his rifle in his hands pointing at them. Red Boynton blustered, "Marshal, we ain't done nothing wrong. We're just here to work for the Double B, so you got no cause to gang up on us this way!" Brian gave him a grim smile as Mark came up to stand with him, facing them. "We ain't ganging up on you," he told Red. "It's two against two, although I know that you are more of a bushwhacker and are too scared to actually face a man!" Mark said, "Actually, to call you a bush-whacker is to give a bushwhacker a bad name! You two are just yellow-bellies, and you sure don't look like brothers! Do either of you know your father?" Blaze Boynton snarled and went for his gun, and so did Red. Brian palmed his gun and shot Blaze who had his pistol halfway out of his holster. Mark just tilted the rifle barrel and shot Red Boynton as soon as his hand touched his gun butt. One of the men in the saloon went over to check on the Boyntons and said, "Both shot through the heart! They're dead all right!"

In the Marshal's office, Paul Lee asked Brian, "Way I heard it was that you provoked them and forced them to draw?" Brian shrugged and said, "We heard that they never fight fair and were not above bushwhacking their targets, so we figured we would force them to fight fair for once!" Mark said mildly, "I guess they didn't quite stack up to their reputations." Just then Trent Williams walked in and said, "Marshal, we got word that the Boyntons will be coming in today!" He turned to Mark and said, "Harry has men watching the trails, and he got the word and sent me to warn you." Paul Lee said wryly, "You're too late! They came in, and they're here to stay!" Trent looked confused, and Paul told him, "They're on their way to Boot Hill. They ran into the Baileys at the Bison Head." Trent looked shocked and exclaimed, "They're dead?!" Mark said mildly, "Usual practice as I know it is to only plant dead men in Boot Hill."

Trent shook his head and exclaimed, "Man! Am I glad you boys came to town when you did!" He hesitated a bit, and Paul Lee said, "Sit down, Trent. I can see that there's something more on your mind." He sat down and spoke to Brian, "When Baker started bringing in gunmen, Harry sent word to some of his friends to keep a watch and to let him know if gunmen were being hired. He didn't get word about the Boyntons and Black Dave, but yesterday he received a message that Baker has a man out there recruiting gunmen, and so far he has recruited around a dozen. Some of them are outlaws or borderline outlaws, but most are just professional hired guns. They are being recruited from all over: from Nevada, Utah, Colorado, and Kansas. Harry thought you should know what you're up against if you stay on here as deputies." Mark asked him, "What does Harry want us to do?" Trent looked uncomfortable but said, "He told me to tell you to leave town. He said it wasn't fair to keep you involved in a fight in which you had no stake!" Mark said emphatically, "We're not leaving!" Trent looked at Brian and said, "Well, I told you what Harry said."

Brian had seemed to be deep in thought as Trent was speaking, and now he looked up and asked him, "Yes, that's what Harry said, but what do you say? You want us to stay or leave?" Trent again looked uncomfortable, but then he looked Brian straight in the eyes and said, "Me and most of the boys have seen trouble, so we're not greenhorns. We've fought Indians, we've been over the trail and back, we've had our fair share of gunfights, but we've no experience for a war like this! So I would like you to stay on, even if that seems mighty selfish!" Brian smiled and said, "I like a straight-talking man! We'll be staying, and tomorrow morning I would like Harry and you to come to town, and I'll lay out my plan of action." Trent left, and Paul Lee told Brian, "You know, Harry's right. You boys don't have a stake in this, and it's unfair of us to get you involved!" Brian laughed and remarked, "Maybe Mark thinks he has a stake in this!" Pretending to be shocked, Mark asked him, "What are you talking about! What stake?" Brian laughed again and told him, "I ain't blind, kid! At the Box T you were hard put to it to keep your eyes away from Sally Taylor!" Mark blustered and then got red in the face, while Brian and Paul laughed. "You couldn't do better, Mark," Paul said. "That's a fine upstanding young girl, and without a doubt she's a beauty!"

CHAPTER 3
THE PLAN

THE NEXT MORNING, HARRY, TRENT, AND RICK WERE seated in the Marshal's office with Paul Lee, Brian, and Mark. Brian was speaking and he told Harry, "What you did with the dynamite when the Double B drove in those cattle was a good plan. Now I want you to do the same for your ranch house, just in case they attack you there in force." He went on to tell them about the Cedar Creek battle and how the Double M and the Rafter K had defended their ranch houses from an attack by superior forces. "Place distinctive markers as rangefinders so your riflemen will be able to call their shots more accurately. Don't connect the dynamite fuses until an attack is actually underway, to prevent any accident. Just keep the ends in a safe but accessible place, and make sure the wires are buried deep enough so that they can't be accidentally cut. Always keep five men at the ranch house and have two men watching the boundary line. The rest can go about their normal daily work."

"What about the town?" Rick asked. "What if they attack the town?" Mark said, "That's unlikely, although one can never say for sure, but in any case, we've alerted the townspeople to the danger and they will be armed at all times. We've a core group of ten men and they've been told what to do in the event of an attack." Brian said, "We've taken precautions, but we don't think they will attack the town. It isn't easy to tree a western town, as some dime novels would have you believe. In a western town, almost everyone carries a gun, and more importantly, they know how to use those guns. In any western town, you will find Indian fighters, old buffalo hunters, and war veterans; and they will all fight at the drop of a hat, and sometimes drop the hat themselves!"

He then told Harry, "Every morning Mark will ride out to the Box T and take a look around the range, especially the boundary line between the Box T and the Double B." He paused and then added, "We'll wait for them to make a move or at least for those hired guns to get here. Maybe what happened with the Boyntons has given Baker some food for thought." Harry said, "That man will never change!" But Brian said, "I don't know, there for a time he seemed to hesitate, as though he had some doubts when I laid out his actual troubles for him. But as I told Paul, then Len Spalding spoke, and Baker's arrogance reasserted itself, and he warned us and rode off." They left it at that, and the Box T men went back to the ranch. Mark asked Brian, "What was that about me going to the Box T every morning?" Brian laughed, and slapping his brother on his back, he said, "How else are you going to get to see that girl with a war going on, kid?"

The next morning, Mark rode to the Box T and waited in the front yard for Trent Williams. Sally came out and called to him, "Come on in for some coffee and breakfast if you haven't eaten as yet." Mark mumbled, "Thanks, but I've got a lot of range to cover; just waiting on Trent to come with me." Sally put her hands on her hips and said, "Well, you can wait for Trent while you have some coffee, or don't you think I can make good coffee?" Mark was immediately off his horse, saying, "Of course not, Miss. I bet you make real good coffee." As he walked up to her, she said, "And my name isn't Miss, its Sally!" Mark raised his hands in surrender and said, "Okay, Sally, I'd love to have some coffee!" She laughed, and they both walked into the house. Her mother, Ruth, who had been watching the exchange from inside, smiled to herself.

Mark sat down at the dinner table and Sally poured him a cup of coffee. "Rick tells me that your family are the Baileys who were involved in the Cedar Creek battle in Texas," she told Mark, who just nodded in agreement. "So, is this fight somewhat like what happened over there?" she continued. "I mean, we heard that over there they had also hired a lot of gunfighters, just like Bart Baker is doing here right now." Mark said, "Yes, I guess so. Say, this is really mighty fine coffee!" Sally gave him a thoughtful look and asked him, "Are you changing the subject because you don't like to talk about that fight, or is it that you think a girl shouldn't know anything about fighting?"

It was now Mark who gave her a thoughtful look, and he said, "Actually, I suppose I just figured you were too young and must be leading a very sheltered life here." Sally said indignantly, "I am not too..." But before she could complete what she was going to say, Mark again raised his hands in surrender and said, "Which I can see was something that was really stupid of me to think! Your father is too savvy a man to keep his daughter away from the realities of this harsh frontier life." Sally again began to say something, but Mark cut her off by saying, "And of course you're not too young! My sister Betsy was a sharpshooter with a rifle at the age of 12, and before that, when we were on our way to Texas from Tennessee, she would load the weapons during an Indian attack." Sally forgot to be indignant and asked him, "Your family is back in Texas?"

"Yes," said Mark. "My Pa, my eldest brother Mike, my youngest brother Luke, and of course my sister Betsy, who is married to Bruce McCullough."

"So why are you and your brother travelling right now?" Sally asked him. Mark shrugged, "We figured to raise a stake in the Arizona goldfields and then start ranching on our own." Sally asked him, "Your Ma is not alive?" Mark told her, "When we were on our way to Texas to start ranching, she was killed during an Indian attack, and so she never saw Texas."

"Oh! I'm so sorry!" Sally cried. "It's okay," Mark said. "That was ten years ago, and we named the ranch the Rafter K in her honor. Her name was Kate." Just then, Trent Williams walked in and said, "You ready to go, Mark?" Mark got up and told Sally, "It was nice talking to you. Maybe I'll see you again?" Sally smiled and told him, "I'm not going anywhere, so I hope you'll visit again when you don't have 'so much range to cover.'" Mark laughed and went out with Trent Williams.

They were riding towards the boundary line when suddenly Mark pulled up, and pointing to a high-looking butte in the distance, he asked Trent, "Has anyone been up there?" Trent shaded his eyes from the sun and looked where Mark was pointing. "I don't think so," he said. "Why?" Mark told him, "I would say that that is less than two miles from the Double B ranch house, so let's go there." When they came to the butte, Mark saw that it was actually higher than it looked from a distance, and he rode around searching for a way to the top. They found what looked like an old Indian trail which was partly grown over with shrubs and covered with fallen boulders. They urged their horses forward and went up the slope, being careful not to disturb any boulders.

They finally came to a broad ledge, and from there the horses could go no further. Mark hung a pair of army field glasses from his neck, and taking a lariat from Trent, he slung it over his shoulder and began climbing to the top. Stepping from boulder to boulder and clinging on to shrubs, he eventually made it to the top, which he found to be quite flat. He walked to the edge, and using the field glasses, he looked towards where he figured the Double B ranch house would be. He was surprised when the ranch house sprang into focus, because the entire area around it was clear through the field glasses and he could see the horses in the corral, and he saw a man ride up to the house and Baker coming out to meet with him.

Taking the lariat, he tied one end securely to a large boulder and then dropped the other end towards Trent and told him to climb up. When Trent came up, he showed him the view of the Double B through the field glasses and told him, "Put a man up here at all times during the day to keep a watch on what's happening over there." Trent was impressed and said, "That was good thinking, Mark! We never really thought of this butte as a lookout point since it's so far away." Mark shrugged and said, "Without the field glasses, it's no use as a lookout point. Brian gave me the glasses and told me to search for a high point within two miles of the Double B, because that's the extent of the glasses' reach." Leaving the lariat where it was, Trent rode back to the ranch to arrange matters, and Mark headed back to town.

The next morning he told Brian, "I think you had better head to the Box T today and check out that lookout point that Trent should have set up by now." Brian gave him a curious look and asked, "Things go okay with Sally yesterday?" "Of course," Mark replied. "We spoke, and in fact, she will be expecting me today. But you can tell her why you are there and say that I'll be coming in tomorrow." Brian gave him a thoughtful look, but Mark was already moving away and said over his shoulder, "I'll take a ride around the town, and I'll talk to Paul about keeping someone to watch the trails leading to town." But when Brian rode out of town, he was still thoughtful and a bit puzzled that Mark did not want to go to the Box T today. When he reached the Box T, Sally came running out of the front door, and it was obvious to Brian that she was disappointed to see him. He was seated at the table and she had served him coffee when he asked her, "I'm not trying to be inquisitive, and there's a reason for me asking, but did things between you and Mark go well yesterday?" Sally looked puzzled, and she said, "We spoke, and he said that he would be coming today. I can't think why he wouldn't have come."

Brian looked worried and stood up. "Where's Trent?" he asked her. "Right here," said Trent, who had just come in the front door. "When did you place a lookout on top of that butte?" Brian asked him. "Yesterday," Trent replied. "As soon as I got back here."

"The man you sent yesterday," he asked Trent. "Is he here now, and could I talk to him?"

"Of course," Trent replied. He went to the front door and shouted, "Reese! Come over here right now!" A tall, gangling cowboy came running from the bunkhouse. "What is it, boss?" he asked Trent. Brian had come to the front door, and he told him, "Tell me what you saw during your watch of the Double B yesterday." Reese thought for a moment and then said, "Like I told the boss, I saw five men ride in who looked like hired guns to me." Brian was impatient and said brusquely, "Anything else? I need you to tell me everything that you saw. For instance, did you see Baker?" Reese frowned in thought and then said, "Yes, he was standing with another man when these men rode in, and it looked to me like the other man was doing the talking." Brian said, and there was an urgency in his voice now, which surprised Trent and Reese, "Describe this man!" Reese frowned again and then said, "Well, it's difficult at that distance, but he looked taller than Baker, so he would be over six feet. I'm pretty sure that he had a full beard and whiskers to boot!" Brian asked sharply, "What color was his beard?" Reese looked at him in confusion and said, "Well, black, it was black!" Brian immediately started for his horse, and Trent said, "Brian, I'm in the dark here! Tell me what's on your mind!" Brian swung into the saddle and said, "I can't be sure, but I think that that there man is Black Dave, going by the description that Paul gave us." He turned his mount and said, "I think that's the reason why Mark stayed in town today. I've got to go!" He rode away, and Trent shouted at Reese, "Round up the boys right now, we're riding to town!"

CHAPTER 4
THE RED BUTTE CREEK WAR

MARK HAD BEEN SURE THAT THE MAN HE HAD SEEN through the field glasses was Black Dave. He had sent Brian out of town because he had decided to face Black Dave himself. It wasn't bravado, but simply the fact that he knew he was faster than Brian, and given Black Dave's reputation, he figured he should be the one to face him. After Brian left, he put two men to watch the trails leading to the town, and giving them a description of Black Dave, he told them to get word to him immediately if they saw the man coming to town. It was an hour later and he was in the Bison Head when one of the lookouts came running in and told him, "A man of that description is riding in and he should be here in ten minutes." Mark asked him, "Is he alone?" The man said he was, and Mark thanked him and told him to go back and watch if more men were coming in. "Don't let them see you," he told the man. Pat Fields asked him, "What's happening, Mark?" Mark shrugged and told him, "I think that might be Black Dave. You get the men together just in case more hired guns come in behind him." Pat Fields looked worried and said, "You going to face him alone? Let me get the men together and we'll just arrest him." Mark shook his head and declared, "If he's alone, then I'll face him alone. You get the men and watch my back!" He walked out of the saloon and stood on the boardwalk, leaning against a pole with his rifle in his hands. The only thing he did was to loosen the gun in his holster as he waited.

The tall, bearded man rode slowly up the street, and Mark called out, "Stop right there and get off your horse!" The man looked at Mark and noted the badge and the rifle in his hands, which was pointing at him. He got down off his horse and slowly walked towards Mark, who had stepped off the board-walk and stood waiting in front of the saloon. The man stopped ten feet away and said, "What's the matter, Marshal? You in the habit of stopping strangers who ride into town?" Mark asked him bluntly, "Are you Black Dave?" The man stared at Mark for a moment and then said, "I'm Dave Schwartz and I hear tell that they call me Black Dave." Mark leaned the rifle against the pole and took two steps towards the center of the street. "And I hear tell that you've been hired by the Double B to do some killing," Mark told him. Black Dave shrugged and said with a grim smile, "Maybe so, but I wasn't told to kill no Marshal!" Mark told him, "You got two choices. You can mount up and ride out of here without stopping until you're out of the territory, or you can draw right now."

Black Dave suddenly turned serious and he looked at Mark carefully. "You sure about that, Marshal?" he asked. "You think you can take me?" Mark said mildly, "We won't know until it's over. You still got a choice to make." Without another word, Black Dave drew and his gun was sweeping up when a shot rang out and he staggered back. Mark had palmed his gun in a move that Pat Fields, who was watching from the saloon, would later say that he never really saw Mark's hand move, but just the blast from the gun. As Black Dave staggered back, he raised his gun again and dropped the hammer, but Mark was walking forward and he triggered another shot that took Black Dave through the heart, and the bullet from Dave's gun went into the ground two feet in front of Mark. Black Dave slowly crumpled and lay still in the dusty street with the gun still held in his hand. Mark walked forward slowly, keeping a wary eye on the still form, and then kicked the gun from Dave's hand. Only then did he bend down to check on Dave. He straightened up as Pat Fields came running and all he said was, "He's dead." Suddenly there was the pounding of hooves of a fast-running horse and Mark swung around to see Brian charging down the street.

Brian and Mark were sitting at a table in the Bison Head and Brian was saying, "Don't ever do something like that again, Mark! I should have been here to back you up." Mark gave him a level look and said, "He was really fast, Brian! Jack taught us that concentration technique that helps a person to move really fast and I've been practicing it constantly. I know you haven't, but I have." He held up his hand as Brian started to speak and said, "I've been practicing and it actually works, and I know that I'm faster than I've ever been!" He sighed and then continued, "He got his gun out, Brian. He got his gun out and he had it aimed when I shot him. He staggered and I shot him again but he still managed to get off a shot which went into the ground. He was very fast, Brian, very fast!" Brian touched his shoulder and said, "But you got him, Mark. You got him, and when we see Jack again I'll thank him for saving your life. But don't ever face anything again without me. Understood?" Mark gave a shaky laugh and said, "You got it, big brother. Now let's go to the Marshal's office and make a plan."

They walked out of the saloon to find the street lined with Box T riders. "Trent!" Brian said. "You come with us. The rest of you boys can hole up in the Bison Head." Seated in the Marshal's office, Brian told them about Reese seeing more gunmen at the Double B. Paul Lee asked him, "So what's the plan?" Brian said, "I think it's time that we paid the Double B a visit." Trent hesitated and said, "What if more gunmen have come in by now? They could easily outnumber us." It was Mark who told him, "We're going to whittle their numbers down. We're not going to charge in with guns blazing, we're going to surround them and take them out one by one; with rifles!" Trent said, "Except for a few of us, the rest aren't really what you could call sharpshooters." Brian smiled grimly, "We are! The Baileys' weapon of choice is actually the rifle and not the six-gun." Mark added, "We surround them and your boys will be there to make sure they don't make a break for it. We'll do the sharpshooting!"

There were eight riders of the Box T, including Trent, and they rode with the Bailey brothers to the Double B after making a stop at the Box T. Harry and Rick wanted to join the attacking force, but Mark told them to stay put with the remaining cowboys in case an attack was launched by the Double B. On reaching the Double B, Brian placed the men at strategic points with ample cover and he and Mark took up positions on opposite sides of the ranch house. Brian held a short discussion with Trent and told him what to do. Then Brian shouted, "Baker! This is the deputy Marshal! Tell your men to throw out their guns and come out with their hands held high!" For an answer, several shots were fired in the direction of his voice, but Brian was safe behind a tree. No shots were fired in return as Brian had given strict instructions to the Box T crew on what to do and what not to do. There was a lull, but Brian was waiting for Trent to carry out his instructions. After about ten minutes, a face appeared at the bunkhouse window, as did a face at a window of the ranch house. Brian and Mark's rifles spoke and the faces disappeared.

There were yells and curses from the bunkhouse and the ranch house. Trent came up behind Brian and said, "We're ready for the signal." Brian shouted again, "You men in there! We know you're hired guns, but the cost of fighting just went up. You have one minute to surrender!" There was no answer and after exactly a minute, Brian triggered two fast shots from his pistol. Immediately, there were two loud explosions from the back of the bunkhouse and the back of the ranch house that shook the buildings. Brian had picked up some dynamite from the Box T and the cowboys had crept up to the back of the buildings and placed the charges. The explosions ripped huge portions off the walls and the Box T riders poured a hail of lead into the buildings. There was a sudden deafening silence once the guns stopped and Brian shouted, "Last chance and you won't get another! We've more charges placed and once we detonate those nothing will be left of you men!" There was loud cursing and then a voice called out from the bunkhouse, "Hold it! We're coming out!"Brian shouted in reply, "Guns first and then come out with your hands held high. Any sudden moves and we shoot to kill."

Rifles and pistols were thrown out from the bunkhouse and then five men came out with their hands in the air. Mark shouted, "Move to your left towards those trees and don't stop until you're told to do so!" The men did as they were told and once they were in the grove of trees, the Box T riders tied them up. Brian called out, "You there in the ranch house; last chance!" A fusillade of bullets was the answer. As per Brian's plan, Mark had made his way to the back of the house which had been blown up. He had with him a slingshot and two sticks of dynamite. What he was going to do was dangerous, but he was confident he could pull it off. Placing a stick of dynamite in the slingshot, he lit the fuse. Then he carefully wound up his arm and in one smooth move he let go, and the dynamite went sailing through the broken wall to explode deep inside the house. A few seconds later, the next stick of dynamite landed and exploded. There were yells and curses, and guns came flying out of the ranch house followed by men running with their hands in the air. "Hold it there!" Brian shouted. "Everyone lie face down in a line with your hands behind your back. Do it now!"

The men complied, but Brian was looking for Bart Baker and he did not see him. "Where's Baker?" he asked the men. One of them raised his head and said, "He left with ten men to take the town. We were just getting ready to ride to attack the Box T." Trent and his boys quickly tied up the rest of the gunmen, and after tying them to their saddles, the whole cavalcade rode to town. At the outskirts of the town, they placed the tied-up gunmen on the ground and left two cowboys to guard them. The rest split up into two groups of four, with Brian leading one group and Mark the other. They circled the town from opposite sides and silently moved in between the buildings. Brian and his group went to the Marshal's office and Mark and his group went to the Bison Head. Taking a peek through the windows, they saw that there were six men in the Bison Head and five in the Marshal's office, which included Baker.

Brian positioned one man each at the two windows of the Marshal's office while he and Trent stood at the front door. The two men at the windows opened fire and immediately Brian and Trent burst in through the front door with guns drawn and blazing. It was over in seconds, with three men dead and Baker and another man wounded. Mark had also executed the same plan, and as soon as the shooting at the Marshal's office started, his two men at the windows of the Bison Head opened fire and Mark and Reese burst in through the batwings with their guns firing. The confusion was complete with the simultaneous attacks, and in the Bison Head there were four dead and two wounded. One of the dead men was Len Spalding. The Red Butte Creek War was over.

Baker recovered from his wounds, sold the Double B to Harry Taylor, and left the Territory. It must be said that Harry Taylor gave him a fair price and then went about legally laying claim to the range. Sally and Mark were sitting halfway up the side of a butte under the shade of some stunted trees. "They are saying you are one of the fastest guns in the West," Sally told him. Mark asked her, "Will that be a problem for you?" She gave him a quizzical look and said, "Why should it? I'm a girl of these western lands, Mark, and I know that sometimes guns are the only way to lay down the law." Mark sighed and after a moment he said, "I'll be going now to Arizona. But once we have our stake and start our ranch, would you be willing to marry me?" Sally laughed, "I'm willing right now, Mark. I don't know why you have to go to Arizona when my father is willing to give the Double B range to us to start our own ranch." Mark smiled at her and said, "I'll get that stake and start my own ranch and then I'll come back." He paused, then laughed and said, "It's not as though you were getting to be an old maid! You're just sixteen!" She punched his arm but then said seriously, "You just make sure that you come back to me, Mark Bailey. Try not to get shot because I'll be waiting for you."

CHAPTER 5
TALLY STEVENS

BRIAN AND MARK RODE TO THE GILA RIVER, WHERE their family had made their stake years ago, but the boomtown had been washed out in a flood in 1862. They crossed the river and continued on until they reached the Salt River. They were camped for the night not far from the river, eating a meal of sourdough bread fried with bacon and washed down by strong black coffee.

"Hello the fire," a voice called out from the darkness. "Can I come in?" Nobody rode up to a camp unannounced, as it was an easy way to get shot. Brian said, "Come in if you're friendly, and if you're not, then my rifle will take care of it." An old prospector on a burro rode in slowly until he was within the light from the fire. Then, just as slowly, he swung down and left the burro ground hitched. He chuckled when he saw the rifle in Mark's hand. Mark was sitting at the edge of the firelight and was just a shadow in the night.

"Good move, that," he told Brian. "Any unfriendly would be concentrating on you." He came up to the fire and said, "The smell of that there bacon and coffee drew me in. I'll swap a haunch of prime venison for a taste of that!" Brian smiled and told him, "Sit down and help yourself, we'll fry some more."

The old man said, "Thankee kindly, youngster, it's been a while since I had me some bacon! Ran out of coffee a month ago, I think!" He went to the burro, dug around in his saddle-bags, and came back with a tin plate and cup. He sat down and concentrated on his eating.

When he had finished, he put his plate aside and held out his cup, which Brian filled to the brim. He finished half the cup and then sighed contentedly. "My moniker is Tally Stevens, and I'm what they call a die-hard prospector. It ain't the money but the finding of the ore and taking it out that drives me. Where are you youngsters off to?" Brian told him, "I'm Brian, and this here is my brother, Mark. We heard tell that there's gold to be found near the Little Colorado River, so we're headed there." The old man pondered and then said, "You don't have to go that far. Near Clear Creek there's gold, and there's quite a few miners there already. But they haven't yet found it all, so you could get yourself set up over there. Know anything of prospecting for gold or silver?" Brian shrugged and replied, "Not much, although years back our family made us a good stake from the Gila River gold rush and we started a ranch in Texas."

Tally Stevens scratched his head and asked him, "So if you already have your ranch, why hunt for gold again?" Mark told him, "We're four brothers and one sister, and the ranch won't support us all once we have families of our own, so we thought we'd raise a stake and start our own ranch." Tally scratched his head and pondered for a while.

"You boys were mighty free in sharing the bacon and coffee with an old coot like me, so I'll tell you what I'll do," he told them. "I'll come with you and find you a good claim, and we'll split the take fifty-fifty. You pay expenses for food and equip-ment now, and when we divvy up, I'll pay my share of those expenses." Brian and Mark looked at each other, and Mark said, "It's a deal!" Tally Stevens looked at Brian and said, "So you're the canny one in the family." He told Mark, "No offence, but when you get an offer, you first got to study her from here to yonder and then back again before you say aye or nay. That's what your brother is doing right now!" Brian smiled and said, "We'll take you up on that offer." He held out his hand and said, "Partners?" Tally shook his hand and said, "Pards!"

The next morning they set out, and had been riding for more than two hours when Tally Stevens suddenly pulled up and said, "Boys, you've been decent to me, so I got to come clean. I can't let you ride into Purgatory without fair warning!" Brian pointed to some trees a little distance away and said, "That looks like a good place to stop and have some coffee. Let's go!" He rode away, and Mark and Tally followed him.

With the water on the boil, Brian said, "Okay, Stevens, let's hear it, all of it!" Tally Stevens nodded and said, "You knew something was up!" It was a statement and not a question, and Brian just nodded in agreement. "A canny one," Tally said. "I can still spot 'em!" He waited for a moment, but Brian didn't speak. "I'm just curious, youngster," Tally told Brian. "What gave me away?" Brian sighed and said, "No one is going to give away half his claim just for a taste of bacon and coffee. So it had to have something to do with our name."

Tally said, "But you didn't say your family name. You just said Brian and Mark." Brian shrugged and told him, "You came up with that offer after you spotted the brands on our horses." Tally Stevens gave a rueful smile and said, "I'll say it again, a right canny man!" Neither Brian nor Mark said anything, so he continued, "I've heard of the Rafter K and the Bailey family. In fact, I knew about your father, Nolan, long before you were born. I'm originally from Tennessee, and I know about the Bailey-Hawkes feud, and lately I heard about the Cedar Creek battle. Before that, I heard the tale about the range war in

Kansas and about the fourteen-year-old boy who ended it with a bullet."

He looked at Brian and said, "I'm guessing that would be you?" Brian nodded, and Stevens went on, "Here's the truth about Purgatory. That's the name I gave the place when I found the gold and staked my claim."

Tally Stevens and three other prospectors had found gold in a canyon that branched off from a fertile valley. It was an arid land with red sandstone and sloping, boulder-covered hillsides. Tally figured that comparing this land to the valley they had just crossed would make the valley heaven, and this long canyon would be purgatory, and so that's what they named it. They staked their claims and worked them, and they took out a good quantity of gold. Two of the prospectors were sent to the nearest town of Rockville for supplies and to check in the gold at the assayer's office. Tally Stevens and the other man, who went by the name of Simon Beamon, waited for more than two weeks, but the two prospectors did not return. In anticipation of the trouble that they were sure was coming, they built a wall for protection and cleared the area before their two claims to have a clear field of fire.

Then one day, twenty men rode into the canyon, and when they came within twenty feet of the claim, Tally shouted out, "That's far enough!" The men drew up sharply, and a tall, well-built man riding a fine steel-dust gelding, who was obviously the leader of the group, spoke up, "We didn't know that anyone was here. We're just prospectors, and we're here to file on some claims." Tally said, "And what happened to our two friends who went to Rockville?" The man shrugged and replied, "My name is Josh Williams, and I heard of this find from an old man I found on the trail to Rockville. He had been shot, and he was dying, and I cared for him. In return, he told me about this here find, and so I rounded up some friends and here we are."

Tally said, "It's a free land, so you go ahead and stake your claims, just not the four you see that are already staked!" Josh Williams said, "That old man gave over his claim to me, so I'd be obliged if you could point it out." Tally told him, "That old man didn't have the sole right to any claim. This here is a partnership, so you go file your own claim. What was that man's name again?" Josh Williams smiled, and it was not a nice smile. "I didn't say," he said. "Well boys, let's go stake out our claims."

Tally Stevens told Brian, "I knew that skunk was lying because neither Rolly nor Billy would ever sell out a partnership, and neither would leave the other to die on the trail like that." He paused and then said, "No, I think that this here Josh Williams spotted them in town with the gold and then murdered them after torturing them for the information about the find. Williams was surprised to find us forted up there, so obviously our friends didn't tell him about us." He paused again, and Mark asked, "So what happened after they staked out their claims?" Tally sighed, "Ten of the men were there to find gold. I think that the word got out, and Williams could do nothing to stop them from coming. But the other men were with Williams, and they were there to do some claim jumping if the others found gold!"

Josh Williams and the nine men he had brought along went to the valley and started what they called the town of Providence. They had brought along two wagonloads of goods and moonshine whiskey, and near a stream, they quickly set up a saloon and a store. Both were patchwork affairs and not built to last, but then, Josh Williams did not plan to hang around for long. The other ten men staked out their claims and worked them, and it didn't take long for Tally Stevens to know that they were genuine miners. They got to talking, and the men said that one of Williams' crew had let slip the information of where they were headed when he was drunk in a saloon. The ten miners had followed them, and when they were in the valley, they had made their presence known but with their rifles in their hands.

Williams was not pleased, but then suddenly seemed to accept the situation and told the miners that they were welcome to file their own claims.

"When they told me that," said Tally, "I just knew that Williams was a claim jumper, and I told the miners to be on their guard. One morning, we woke up to find that one of the miners was missing, and sitting on his claim was one of Williams' crew." He sighed and told the Baileys, "Josh Williams and most of his men wear their guns slung low and tied down, and they have the look of real hard men. Williams is the leader and planner, and he's quite a good-looking man, even if he has a pair of sly-looking eyes!"

The other miners demanded to know what had happened to their friend, and Josh Williams came out from the claim and said, "Well, he didn't like the climate, he said, so he sold out to this man here and said that he was hightailing it to Rockville." One of the miners said, "I don't believe it!" Suddenly there was a gun in Williams' hand, and he said softly, "Are you calling me a liar?" Tally Stevens noted that the other men, who had appeared at the back of Williams as he was speaking, were just a shade behind him in the speed of their draw, and now they all held guns in their hands. The miners weren't gunfighters, and they backed off. Later, they held a conference, and it was decided to defend what they could collectively, because by themselves, individually, they would just be knocked off one by one by Williams' crew.

"We're holding on to five claims because they are next to each other," Tally told Brian. "We've built ramparts, and while some work, the others stand guard. They elected me to ride out in the middle of the night to find us some help." He looked at Mark and said, "It was really the smell of the bacon and coffee that made me come to your camp, but when I saw the brand on your horses and I looked at you, I knew you were the answer to my prayers."

Mark was curious and asked him, "What do you mean, when you looked at us?"

Tally smiled and told him, "You've got the Bailey look, and I've seen quite a few Baileys in Tennessee!" Brian was looking thoughtful, and Tally told him, "I was being honest when I said we would be partners. That deal stands! I just couldn't let you ride into that place without knowing what to expect." He waited, but Brian was still thinking, so he said, "Guess what I'm saying is, will you help us?"

It was Mark who asked him, "There really is gold there, or did you just make that up as well?"

Tally held up his hand and said, "There's a lot of gold there, I can promise you that!" Brian stood up and said, "Let's move, we're wasting time!" Tally stood up also and asked him, "So will you help us out?" Brian said, "Let's hope they've managed to hold out. When we reach that there valley, you go your way and we'll check out this town of Providence." Tally said, "When I left there, I passed by that town, and there were at least five more men there than before."

Mark asked, "So Williams is bringing in more guns?"

Brian told him, "Well, when the miners forted up, he must have sent a man to bring in more men. He can't take the miners with just nine men, not if they have cover and they have their rifles. In that situation, being quick on the draw ain't going to help at all!"

CHAPTER 6
PROVIDENCE

WHEN THEY REACHED THE VALLEY, TALLY GAVE THEM directions to the town and to the canyon and then left them to sneak his way back to his claim in the night. The Baileys camped out that night and rode into the town of Providence early the next morning. There were now five other buildings besides the original patchwork saloon and store. The name painted on the saloon was the Providence Saloon and the store was named the Providence Store. There were quite a few men moving around the town, and Brian noted that most of them looked like miners and not gunslingers. The five new buildings were rough but built well, and there was a Lost Mine Saloon, a store, an eatery, and an assayer's office. The last building boasted of being a hotel and offered beds for rent. They tied their horses to the hitching rail in front of the Lost Mine Saloon and walked into the bar. The barkeep was a tough-looking, bald-headed man with huge biceps and a barrel body. He swiped the bar with a rag and asked the brothers, "What'll it be, gents?" Brian smiled and looked around the room and asked, "You mean there's a choice?" The barkeep did not smile and said, "Rye or bourbon.

For moonshine you got to go to that other place." Brian said, "Two shots of rye, please."

When the barkeep had poured the whiskey, Brian told him, "That wasn't meant the way it sounded. It's just that, in this out-of-the-way place, I was surprised that we had a choice of whiskey! Anyone can see that this town has just sprung up; the logs of the buildings are still green." The barkeep seemed pleased and said, "Wherever I go, I offer a choice, and my whiskey is good! I've covered a lot of boom towns, but I don't know about this one!" Mark immediately said, "We heard they're finding gold out there, and we saw a few miners when we rode in." The barkeep shrugged and told him, "I go by the name of Baldy Smith, and yes, there's gold out there, but there's a fight going on as well." Brian said, "But you're here, and I saw an assayer's office as well. Besides, we saw quite a few men who looked like miners to me." Baldy Smith nodded and told them, "The miners have filed claims, and they're working them, and they're finding gold. Their claims are all over the place, and they work in pairs. But the word is that the main source of the gold rests with ten claims, and that's what the fight is about. It's said that originally four claims were staked, and that's where the mother lode is. The other six mines are also good, and there are ten men defending five of the claims, including the original four. There's a group of men led by one Josh Williams, who claims to have bought the original four claims from the prospector who staked them out, and he has said that he would drive out the men defending the mine because he is the actual owner." He paused and then continued, "The men who are in control have combined five of the claims as one mine, and that is what they are defending."

Brian asked him, "What's your opinion of this here Josh Williams?" Baldy gave him a level look and said, "A claim jumper if I've ever seen one, and I've seen a lot of them!" Mark said mildly, "You state your opinions very clearly, but what if we were part of Williams' crew?" Baldy gave him a grim smile and said, "Son, I've been over the trail and crossed the mountains a few times, and I've seen my share of hired guns, and you don't stack up to be one!" He suddenly had a thoughtful look on his face, and after a long moment he said, "As I said, you don't stack up to be hired guns, but I would bet my last bottle of whiskey that you're good with guns!" He pondered for a moment and then looked up and said, "I heard a rumor that old Tally Stevens had lit out of here in the middle of the night about ten days ago. He send you boys here?" Brian didn't answer that question but instead he asked Baldy, "What are those miners doing for supplies if they're bottled up at the mine?" Baldy laughed and said, "That Josh Williams may be a big man wherever he comes from, but he knows nothing about these old mountain men. Tally Stevens' old partner, Rack Jones, is holed up at that mine with the others; he comes here in the middle of the night, and I give him supplies to take back. Tally Stevens and his old partner are part Indian and part lobo wolf, and they can get past any guard that Josh Williams places!"

Brian was thinking as he listened to Baldy talk, and now he asked him, "Any of those hired guns at the Providence Saloon now?" Baldy shrugged and replied, "There's always some of them there, early morning or late night, it don't make no difference. They ain't working, they're just waiting to jump that claim, get some gold, and leave!" Brian asked him, "What about that Providence Store?" Baldy said, "I heard that one of Josh Williams' crew runs it, and they're doing good business selling to the miners who are coming in. Word is that they came here first with two heavily laden wagons and set up the saloon and the store." He shook his head and said, "You just can't figure what a man might do! This here Josh Williams could work some claims and take out some gold, and he can make good money with that saloon and that store, but all he wants is easy money!"

Mark was curious and asked him, "The way you've been

running this here Williams down, what you gonna do if he finds out and comes for you?" Baldy smiled and replied, "Son, I got me two loaded shotguns under this bar here and a Winchester Model '66 in the back room. I think I can take care of a few hired guns if they come here hunting me!" Mark smiled in return and told him, "Well, that's good to hear, but if they do come for you, why, you just holler, and we'll come running!" Baldy turned to Brian and asked him, "So what are you boys planning on doing now?" Brian shrugged and said mildly, "Figured we'd go to that store and ask them for supplies for the holed-up miners. Then we might go to that saloon and ask those idle men there to take those supplies up to the mine." Baldy stared at him in surprise for a long moment and then asked in a shocked tone, "You really gonna do that!?" It was Mark who answered him, "He always means what he says!" Then he muttered, "And he calls *me* the trouble hunter!" They left the store with Baldy still looking as though he couldn't believe what he had just heard.

Brian and Mark rode down to the Providence Store, which was just a roughly put-together shack. Mark asked his brother, "What we gonna do?" Brian said, "Pa always said to whittle down the opposition, so that's what we're gonna do." They hitched their horses in front of the store, and Mark adjusted his gun belt to sit more comfortably and said, "Well, let's go do us some whittling." They walked into the store and found three men sitting around sipping whiskey and smoking. The man sitting behind the counter stood up and said, "What can I do for you gents? You're new around here." Brian told him, "We heard that there were some miners holed up in a claim down that canyon, and we figured to buy them some supplies. You know, food and stuff. Figured they must be getting mighty hungry by now!" The other two men stood up, and Mark said softly, "If you boys make a move to draw those guns, I'm gonna have to kill you. I might add that I don't really like shooting people in the morning." Both the men went for their guns, and Mark shot them both. The man behind the counter reached under and brought out a shotgun, but when he looked up, he found himself staring at the gun in Brian's hand. "Now I should shoot you by rights since you've drawn a gun," Brian said mildly. "But I need you to pack up those supplies, so you just set that shotgun down gently and go and pack!"

The man put the shotgun down as gently as a feather dropping and then grabbed a sack and began stuffing cans into it. "Put in four slabs of bacon while you're at it, and two sacks of coffee," Brian told him. He turned to Mark and said, "Thought you didn't like shooting people in the morning!" Mark was watching the door and he shrugged and remarked, "For them, I made an exception!" Just then, two men ran into the store and one of them said, "Mitch! What was the shooting about?" They saw Mark and Brian and stopped as though they had run into a stone wall. They glanced at the two dead men and one of them asked Mark, "You shot them?" Mark seemed to think for a moment and then asked, "What do *you* think?" The man who had spoken snarled, "Think you're funny? You won't last out the day here." Mark shrugged and asked, "Says who?" The man looked puzzled at Mark's attitude and he said, "Josh Williams has twenty guns here and you'll be dead before the end of this day!" Mark asked him, "Those two part of the twenty guns?" The man snarled, "Yeah! And you'll pay for that!" Mark said softly, "So now there are eighteen guns. You want to make that sixteen?"

The two men were wary because neither Mark nor Brian had drawn their guns, and they began to back out of the store. Mark said, "Don't go now, boys, we've got some work for you to do." The men stopped and one of them said, "Work?" Mark said with an indulgent smile as though he was talking to a child, "Yes, work! You know, when men use their hands to do things and maybe they sweat a bit when they do it?" The man looked at his companion and said, "The hell with this!" They both went for their guns, but with their hands still on their gun butts, two shots rang out and they dropped to the floor, dead before they hit it. Brian said sarcastically, "You're making a lot of exceptions this morning, Mark!" Mark shrugged and retorted, "Well, they seemed hell-bent on making the count sixteen!" Brian said, "You think ole Mitch here is part of that sixteen?" The man behind the counter stuttered, "Please...please...mister, don't shoot me!" Brian told him, "Now why would I do that? You see, I need you to take those supplies and go and deliver them to those miners that your boss has holed up in that canyon." He picked up the shotgun and turned to leave, but at the door he said, "And don't come back without delivering it, because if you do then I *will* shoot you!"

They went over to the Providence saloon and as soon as they walked in, the barkeep asked them, "What was that shooting over at the store?" Brian saw three men sitting at a table, but he walked up to the bar and said, "Oh, that was just some hired guns trying to show how fast they were on the draw." The three men stood up and one of them asked, "And?" Mark was facing them and he said, "Well, they just weren't fast enough." The men went for their guns and Brian tilted the shotgun and gave one of them a belly-full of buckshot. In the same movement, he swung the shotgun and smashed it against the barkeep's head. Mark palmed his gun and shot the remaining two men. He turned to Brian and asked, "The barkeep dead?" Brian leaned over the counter and then said, "Nope, looks like he'll have a headache though!"

"That's unlucky," Mark said. Brian looked confused and asked, "The barkeep's headache is unlucky?" Mark retorted, "No! But now they're down to thirteen and that's an unlucky number!" Brian laughed out loud and exclaimed, "Well, let's hope it's unlucky for Josh Williams!" They went out of the saloon and saw the storekeeper standing in front of his store with the sack of supplies and looking hopefully at the saloon. He saw the brothers come out and he hastily mounted his horse and took off out of town. Mark's only comment was, "He sure looked disappointed." They went back to the Lost Mine saloon and asked Baldy, "So where are the rest of Josh Williams' men, and where is Josh Williams himself?" Baldy stared at the two brothers and then asked, "How many?" Mark said, "Seven, which according to what one of those men said, means there are thirteen left." Baldy wiped his bald head and looked worried. "Listen boys," he said. "The rest will be laying siege to the mine, and Josh Williams will be there. But when he gets word of this, he's going to send more men to town to deal with you two." Brian shrugged and told him, "That's what we figured, so we sent the storekeeper with a sack of supplies to the holed-up miners." Mark said, "We just wanted to know if there is any other place in town where some of the hired guns might be." Baldy seemed to be in shock again, and he just stared at them for a long moment and then he swore, "Hell and damnation! You boys are actually inviting him to send men after you?" Brian said mildly, "Ma always used to take the strap to us if we swore when we were kids, so we don't cuss much even now. But we were asking you if there's another place in town where those hired guns might be?" Baldy shook himself as though to wake up from a bad dream and then told Brian, "Who *are* you boys! Those men weren't slouches on the draw and you've taken out seven of them?" Brian shrugged and told him, "To be honest, I just shot one of them with the shotgun. Mark here took out the other six." Mark asked Baldy impatiently, "Another place in town? Could you get to that before more men get here?"

Baldy seemed to be in a daze, but he shook himself again and then said, "That hotel over there. Williams has rented a large room with ten beds in it for his men when they need a break. He himself has a room to himself there whenever he comes into town." Mark asked him, "The owner or the clerk or whoever is there, are they with Williams?" Baldy said, "Sam Laker is the owner and he stays neutral, although with two shotguns under the counter like me." Mark and Brian left the saloon and went over to the Bed and Rest hotel carrying their rifles. They asked Sam Laker, who was at the reception desk, "We'd be obliged if you would point out the room where Josh Williams' gunmen take their rest." Sam looked them over and asked, "You boys responsible for all that shooting I heard?" Mark told him, "Well, I would say that those men were responsible since they drew on us." Laker said, "I don't want any shooting in my hotel."

"There won't be," Brian promised him. Laker looked them over again and then pointed out the room. "There's five of them sleeping there," he told Brian. They walked over to the room and Brian kicked in the door and the brothers walked in with their rifles held ready. Five men were lying on the ground rolled up in their blankets and there were two empty whiskey bottles on a table. The sound of the door smashing open brought the men out of their blankets, but they froze when they saw the two rifles pointing at them. Brian said, "You men get up carefully and walk out of this room in a line. Don't make any sudden moves because I must warn you that I have an itchy trigger finger!" The men cursed and one of them asked, "Who the hell are you?" Ignoring the question, Mark asked him, "What's your name?" The man stared at him and then replied, "Ike Smith, and if you ain't yeller, then face me in the street right now!" Mark sighed and told him, "Okay, get up and pick up your gun and let's go out." The man got up slowly and put on his hat, and then his boots, and finally swung his gun belt around his hips. "After you," Mark told him politely.

The man walked out with Mark following until they reached the street. "Turn around," Mark told him. Ike Smith turned and drew in one swift move, and he died like that, with his gun in his hand. Mark had been holding his rifle in his left hand, and he just tilted the barrel and shot one-handed, but Ike was headed for Boot Hill nonetheless. The remaining men came out of the hotel, flanked by Brian, and they stared at Ike Smith lying dead in the street. Brian told them, "You men have a choice. Either shoot it out here or drop your gun belts and ride south, and don't stop until you hit Mexico." The men looked at each other, then looked again at Ike Smith's body, and one of them told Mark, "You know who that was you just gunned down?" Mark shrugged and said, "He said his name was Ike Smith." The man said sharply, "Ike Smith, the fastest gun in Colorado!" Mark retorted, "Maybe he should have stayed in Colorado!" Brian told them, "Make your choice and make it fast, I ain't a patient man!" The men dropped their gun belts, mounted their horses without speaking, and rode away towards the south. Mark said, "So now Williams has eight men if you can believe the man who said that he had twenty guns." Brian was thoughtful and said, "Tally did say that Williams most probably had sent for more men, so maybe there are more on the way, or they are already at the canyon. I think we better ride and wait under cover at the mouth of that canyon and see what comes out of it."

They rode fast and hard, and on reaching the entrance to the canyon they looked around. Brian went up one slope while Mark went up the opposite side, about ten feet further up from where Brian was. They tied their horses behind some trees, then came back halfway down and took cover behind some boulders with their rifles held ready, and they waited. They had timed it right, for within a few minutes, the storekeeper Mitch and four men came riding up the canyon at a fast pace. When they were near to where Brian was, he put two bullets in the ground in front of their horses and yelled out, "You men want to live, you just stay right where you are and don't go making any sudden moves!" The men started to wheel their horses around, and Mark put two bullets in the ground behind them and yelled, "You heard the man! You want to live, you just stand still." The men cursed but quieted their mounts, because while they couldn't see the shooters, they knew they were on opposite sides of the canyon and had them boxed in.

Brian shouted out, "Now you men just get off your horses and line up in front of them." The men hesitated, and Mark called out, "Either do as he says, or I'll start emptying some saddles! I must warn you that I ain't never missed a shot at this range since I was about knee-high to my daddy!" The men cursed again but got off their horses and lined up in front of them. Brian said, "Now I want you to unbuckle those gun belts and just let them drop!" The men dropped their gun belts, and Brian came out of cover and ran down to the trail. "Lie face down on the ground with your hands behind your backs," he said. One of the men said derisively, "Big man when you got the drop! You're nothing but a lousy bushwhacker!" Brian said, "My Pa always told me that when you see vermin, you just shoot them dead. I ain't shot you yet because I don't know if you fit that category." The man spat on the ground and said, "If you ain't a yeller belly, you'd face me when I had my guns on!" Brian sighed and said mockingly, "Now you're gonna tell me that you're the fastest gun in Utah or someplace else!" The man stared at him and said, "You crazy? I ain't the fastest gun in Utah or anywhere. At least, not that I know of!" Brian palmed his pistol and shot the man in the right hand. "No point in killing you if you ain't the fastest gun from *somewhere*," he said.

Seeing the speed of that draw, the rest of the men lay down on the ground without further protest, except for the man that Brian had shot, who was holding his bleeding right hand and cursing again. Mark came up and tied the men's hands together behind their backs. He then tied a tourniquet around the wounded man's arm to stop the bleeding, then tied his hands together and got him on his horse, where he tied the man's legs together by passing the rope under the belly of the horse. He did the same thing with the other men as well. "Where's those supplies, Mitch?" Brian asked the storekeeper. Mitch replied sullenly, "Josh Williams took them off me." Brian gave him a sad look and said, "Now see, that there's the problem! I told you not to come back if you didn't hand over those supplies to the miners. So now I got to read you from the Good Book!"

He cut the rope from Mitch's legs, and pulling him off his horse he dragged him up the slope behind some boulders, with Mitch protesting all the way. Out of sight of the others, Brian hunkered down, and taking out a knife he told Mitch conversationally, "I brought you here because my brother don't like to see what I can do to a man to get him to talk. I lived for a while among the Apaches, and I learnt from them how to skin a man and still keep him alive." He thought for a moment and then said, "Well, keep him alive for at least three hours. I never seen anyone last longer than that." Mitch stared at him with eyes opened wide in shock and fear. "You don't have to do that," he cried. "What do you want to know...just ask me and I'll...I'll tell you!" Brian seemed to contemplate that, but then shook his head and said, "How would I know if you were lying? Now, the Apache way...that's foolproof, because no man is gonna lie with his skin being slowly stripped away from his body! I hear the pain is really terrible!" Mitch was sobbing now, and he cried, "Please...please...just ask me and I won't lie. I promise you!" Brian asked him, "How many men are there now with Josh Williams? Up at the mine, I mean." Mitch babbled, "Ten...ten... ten men, including Josh." He screamed as Brian pulled his cheek out and placed the knife against his skin. "Ten men, ten men," he cried out. "I'm not lying, you can ask those men, and they'll say the same thing!" Brian replaced his knife, and getting up, he pulled Mitch to his feet and pushed him to start walking down the slope.

After tying the storekeeper to his horse, Brian said, "Now you men are going to ride ahead of us, and when we get to where Williams has his men, you'll tell us. If you don't, then you can just get shot in the crossfire. And don't think of suddenly urging your horse to race away, because you'll be on a lead rope." Mark tied lead ropes to three of the horses, and Brian tied ropes to the remaining two. They rode on, but when they came to a branch in the canyon, Brian pulled up and told Mark, "Let's place them tied up behind those boulders, and we'll just take ole Mitch here to guide us." They left the men but took the horses with them. Mitch was riding ahead of them, and Brian told Mark, "Williams has got ten guns there, including himself, according to Mitch." Mark was curious, "How did you get him to talk? He was screaming, but when you came back, he didn't have a scratch on him!" Brian chuckled, "Told him the old story about how I had lived with Apaches and knew how to skin a man alive! Ole Mitch there sure did believe me!"

Mitch half-turned his body and told Brian, "Just ahead there should be two men on either side of the trail, hunkered down behind some rocks and shrubs. Then you ride a half-mile more, and the rest are spread out on the hillside opposite to the Purgatory mine. They shoot at the mine occasionally, but they are just waiting for a miner to show some part of himself to be shot at." Brian asked him, "Williams should know that he can't do that for much longer, so he has to have a plan. What is it?" Mitch hesitated, and Brian just pulled out his knife and went up to him. Mitch shrank back with real fear in his eyes, and he said, "He's sent for more men, and he's just waiting for them to get here, and then he's going to attack the mine. He's expecting them to arrive tomorrow." Brian tied him to a tree and told Mark, "You take the one on that side and I'll take the one on this side." They split up, and it didn't take them long to find and hog-tie the two men and drag them back to the horses. The men were actually half-asleep when the brothers crept up on them! They tied the two men and the storekeeper to their saddles and rode back to pick up the remaining men. With two horses carrying double, they rode fast for the town of Providence.

Mark asked Brian, "We ain't attacking Williams?" Brian told him, "I've been contemplating on this situation, and I think I've got a better plan." He didn't say anything further until they were back in town and had placed the tied-up men in their room at the Bed and Rest hotel. "Let's go see Baldy Smith," Brian said. At the Lost Mine saloon, Brian asked Baldy, "When does Tally or his partner show up for supplies?" Baldy said, "Usually in the middle of the night." Brian told him, "Me and my brother are going to sleep right here, and I want you to wake us up when Tally or his partner comes in. I need to talk to them."

They were rolled up in their blankets, sleeping in the back room of the saloon, when Baldy walked in. Immediately, both the brothers were awake and sat up with guns in their hands. "Light sleepers," Baldy said. "I like that! Tally Stevens is in the bar having a drink right now." Brian and Mark walked into the bar and Tally Stevens smiled at them and said, "I been hearing that you boys have been waging war against Williams and his hired guns! I'm mighty obliged to you." Brian told him all that had happened since they had ridden into the town the previous morning. Tally said slowly, "Let me try and read this trail! You've been in town for less than twenty-four hours, and you've killed eight of Williams' hired guns, you've sent four of them packing, and you've got another seven tied up at the hotel?" He shook his head in disbelief and said, "When I asked you boys for help, I didn't know I was getting an army!" Brian waved his hand impatiently and said, "Listen, including Josh Williams, there are eight men at the mine now. He's expecting more men to arrive tomorrow, and then he's going for an all-out attack on your mine. Even with your men on the inside of the mine and Mark and me on the outside, that's just too many men to handle."

Tally Stevens said, "So maybe we should sneak up on them in the night and take them out one by one. I've been thinking of doing just that!" Brian disagreed and said, "While that will work out eventually, it will take time, time that you don't have, because Williams is expecting his reinforcements by tomorrow, according to Mitch the storekeeper." Tally Stevens sighed and said, "I know. So what are we going to do?" Brian said softly, "We are going to give them the mine." Tally jumped up and shouted, "What? That ain't never gonna happen! We'll die first before we let that man take our mine!" Brian said mildly, "Sit down, Tally, and listen to my plan." Tally slowly sat back down, and Brian proceeded to lay out his plan.

CHAPTER 7
THE PURGATORY FIGHT

THE NEXT DAY, JOSH WILLIAMS' REINFORCEMENTS arrived, a total of ten men, including the man he had sent to do the recruitment. Together with the men he had left, that made a total of twenty. He fully expected the four men he had sent to town with Mitch and the five men who were on a break in the town to join up with him that night. He was confident that the four men he had sent, together with the five that were already in town, would deal with the two newcomers who had come in and taken out seven of his men. Rod Staver, his second in command, reported to Josh late that morning that the two men on sentry duty had disappeared. Josh Williams was, for the first time, starting to get worried.

"You think they just left?" he asked Staver.

Rod Staver shrugged, "It's possible, I guess, since they weren't of much account, but why would they leave?"

Williams was silent, and Staver said, "Maybe we ought to ride into town with all our men and deal with these two strangers. I can't believe that two drifters could take out seven of our men!"

Williams frowned and asked him, "So what are you saying?"

Staver said, "I'm saying they can't be just ordinary drifters. Maybe the miners have hired someone to fight for them. That Tally Stevens is an old lobo wolf, and he has many friends across the country. What if there are more than two men in town?"

Williams got up and paced around in a circle while he thought. Finally, he said, "Listen, Rod, we now have twenty guns here, and we can take that mine even if the men in town don't turn up tonight. Let's say you're right, and there are more men in town than just those two. We ride in and there will be a gun battle, and even if we win we'll sustain some losses, which will make it harder to take that mine."

Staver asked him, "So what's your plan?"

Williams said, "I say we take the mine tonight. Once we are in possession, then no matter how many guns these miners have brought in, they won't be able to move us out. We'll send Jock out again right now with orders to recruit another twenty men. So if we get trapped in the mine, we only have to hold out till those men arrive. But the main thing would be that we will be in possession!"

Staver said, "And if our men in town don't make it here tonight?"

Williams shrugged and told him, "That would mean that there are more than just two drifters, and taking possession of the mine becomes all the more important!"

Rod Staver stood up and said, "Okay, I'll brief the men, and we attack tonight!"

The men from the town never showed, and late that night, eight men, including Josh Williams, laid down a barrage of gunfire at the mine while the remaining gunmen charged the mine in an attack from two sides. When they reached the ramparts of rocks and dirt that the miners had put up, the eight men ceased firing and rushed to join them. Staver looked over the rock and dirt wall cautiously but could see no one. Signaling to the rest, he climbed over the low wall with his rifle held ready in his hands. Half the men climbed over the wall with him, while the rest stayed behind the wall to provide covering fire. Staver had moved about five feet into the mine when he suddenly stopped and turned around. In a low voice, he told Williams, "Josh, I don't like this! No one seems to be here!"

Before Williams could reply, the silence of the night was again split with the thunder of guns. From the far rock wall behind the mine, guns spoke, and the men with Staver fell. From the built-up ramparts on the slope opposite the mine, which had just been vacated by Williams and his men, guns spoke, and the men with Williams in front of the mine rampart fell. The men on both sides of the rock and dirt wall returned the fire, but they were shooting at shadows while they were caught in a crossfire. As suddenly as it had begun, the shooting stopped and a voice rang out, "You men have one chance! Drop your guns right now and raise your hands high. At the count of five we will open fire again, and this time we won't stop!" The voice began counting, but by the time the count had reached three, ten men had thrown down their guns and raised their hands up in the air. The voice again rang out, "Walk down the slope and lay down in the trail face down." The men complied, except for Josh Williams and Rod Staver, who had dived to the side at the start of the shooting and had found cover behind a large mound of rubble that had been dug out of the mine.

The previous night, after Brian had spoken of his plan to Tally Stevens, the old prospector had gone back to the mine and brought the miners out. They had split their force into two, with one group under the command of Mark going back and laying low under cover a good distance away from the mine but well within the range of their rifles. The other group, under the command of Brian, had circled to the back of the attackers and waited for them to vacate the place when they charged the mine. Brian's plan was simple: to catch the hired guns in a crossfire. In case the men who gave the initial covering fire remained at their stations, then the plan was to attack them first and take them out, and then catch the remaining men in a crossfire. But Brian had figured it right the first time, and all the hired guns had charged up to the mine. Now, with guns trained on the spot where Williams and Staver had taken cover, some of the miners moved down to the men lying on the ground, bound their hands behind their backs, and then marched them up the slope to where Brian was. Mark began shooting to keep Williams and Staver pinned down while Brian ran up to the mine ramparts.

"You've nowhere to go, Josh Williams!" Brian shouted out. "Come out with your hands in the air, or I'm gonna throw these dynamite sticks behind that rubble where you're hiding." He waited for a long moment and then said, "Okay, you made your choice, so I'm lighting these fuses."

"Wait!" Staver shouted. "I'm coming out, don't fire!" He came out slowly with his hands in the air, and Brian could see that he had been wounded just above his hip. After a moment, Josh Williams also came out with his hands raised. Brian pointed his rifle at the two and said, "Walk slowly towards me." Williams and Staver walked towards him, and Mark and his group came up silently behind them.

"You can stand where you are now and don't make no sudden moves because I've got an itchy trigger finger, and I would hate to shoot a man in the back," Mark said in a conversational tone. "Although," he continued, "for you, I'd be willing to make an exception!" They stood still while Mark lifted their guns from their holsters, and a miner retrieved their rifles. Then Mark marched them out of the mine and down to the trail to be tied up like the rest of the hired guns.

Mark told Brian, "There are eight men up there. Five are dead, and the remaining three are wounded. One of the miners is patching up their wounds." With all the gunmen, including Josh Williams, tied to their horses, Brian, Mark, and Tally started for town. They left the rest of the miners at the mine, and Brian told them to stay alert just in case Williams had more men coming in.

They rode into town and dismounted before the Lost Mine saloon. Baldy went to the Bed and Rest hotel and came out with the other seven men. Brian told the gunmen, "You have a choice. You can ride out of here right now without your guns, or we can hold you here by converting the Providence saloon into a jail until the nearest Sheriff can get here and arrest you." One of the men said, "What about our gear?" Brian shook his head and said, "Ride out right now or stay here in jail!" Two of the men said, "Give us a break! We'd be defenseless out there without any guns!"

Mitch cried out, "But what about my store? All my money is in that, and without it, I'm broke!"

Mark shrugged and told him, "You should have thought about that when you hired on to attack miners and jump their claims." The men muttered amongst themselves but then said, "We'll go." Mark gave them a final warning. "And if we see you around here again, then we'll shoot first and ask questions later." The men went to their horses, and Brian cut their bonds one by one and let them mount up and ride. Williams and Staver followed the men, but Mark said, "Not you two! You are staying here!"

Staver asked him, "Why?"

Mark told him, "We know Williams was the boss of this claim-jumping outfit, but we hear that you are his second in command. So you stay here until the Sheriff comes to arrest you for the murder of that miner whose claim you jumped."

Josh Williams had an ugly look on his face, and he told Mark, "Think you're a big man! Give me my guns and face me, and we'll see just how big you are!"

Mark gave him a thoughtful look and said, "We also heard from your hired guns that you are actually a gambler and a killer." Without taking his eyes off Williams, Mark told Brian,

"Cut him loose and give him his guns. Let's see what this bush-whacker is made of!"

The gunmen who were freed were riding out of town but stopped to watch when they heard the challenge. Brian sliced the rawhide strip that was used to tie Williams, and he threw his gun belt on the ground in front of him. Then Brian moved to the side, taking Staver with him, leaving only Mark and Williams facing each other. Josh Williams bent and picked up his gun belt, slung it around his hips, adjusted his holster, and then tied it down while Mark just stood calmly and watched him. Williams finally straightened and, with his right hand hovering over the butt of his six-gun he snarled, "Now you're going to get yours…"

As he was speaking, his left hand jerked, and Mark shot him in the head before he could complete what he was saying. Brian walked over and lifted the dead man's left hand so that everyone could see the derringer hanging down from a spring in his hand. Mark told the others, "I figured he thought that two drifters wouldn't peg him for a man with a sleeve gun, which is why he challenged me. Even so, I waited until his left hand jerked."

Brian said, "Well, he won't be jumping any claims again!" He then turned to Staver and asked him, "How about you? You want to try your luck as well?"

Staver backed off and pleaded, "If it's all the same to you, I'd like to ride out of here, and I promise you won't never see me again!"

Brian cut his bonds and said, "You're lucky I'm in a good mood. Ride, and don't ever come back here!"

The miners celebrated that night in the Lost Mine saloon, and Brian told Tally Stevens, "We'll be riding out in the morning, headed to Colorado."

Tally looked shocked and asked him, "But why? You're a partner now, and you can get a stake right here!"

Brian shrugged and told him, "You have a lot of partners,

and once split so many ways, the stake ain't gonna be that much. At least, not as much as we're looking for! You hold our part of the gold or put it in a bank, and we'll collect it later."

Tally tried to give him a sly look and said, "Sure you can trust me?"

Brian just looked at him, and Tally sighed and said, "Okay, okay, if you've made up your minds, then I guess I can't stop you from leaving. But we'll be here when you do come back, because I'm thinking of making this my last stop. We'll build up this town, and we're renaming it Heaven! The name of the mine, as you know, is Purgatory!"

CHAPTER 8
ANIMAS TOWN

They cut across the south of the Utah Territory and entered the Territory of Colorado. Following the directions of Tally Stevens, they skirted the edge of the Mesa Verde, where they spent a day exploring the cliff dwellings. From there, they rode into the La Plata country. They camped at a stream under a stand of aspen late one afternoon and began to broil some steaks. Suddenly Brian told Mark, "Don't make any sudden moves, but we're being watched!" Mark continued to fill a kettle with water at the stream and asked, "Indians?" Brian said, "I figure they must be the Utes Tally told us about." They sat down by the fire and began eating their steaks while the coffee was on the fire, but their rifles were within easy reach, and they kept a watch without appearing to do so.

After some time, a group of ten Utes rode down the slope and came towards their camp. When they were within twenty feet of the camp, Brian casually picked up his rifle and turned to face them. Raising his left hand with the palm outwards, he said, "Stop! Do my Ute brothers come in peace?" For answer, the Utes nocked their bows, but before the arrows could fly, Brian was behind a tree and firing his Winchester rapidly. Mark wasn't far behind, and his Winchester boomed just a few seconds after Brian had opened fire. Six Indians were down, and at least two more wounded before the Indians realized what was happening. It looked to Brian as though they weren't familiar with a repeating rifle. The remaining Indians turned around and fled, and within minutes Brian and Mark had packed up and were riding hard across a small valley away from the Indians.

They rode into a shanty town, which went by the name of Animas. It consisted mainly of tents and log buildings, but Brian noted that the log buildings actually formed a square with the tents in the center of the square. "They built it so they can fight off an Indian attack," he told Mark. One of the log buildings had the name Animas Saloon painted on it, and the brothers tied their horses at a wooden rail before it, then walked into the room. There was a long bar at one end made up of rough-hewn planks, and a large grey-bearded, balding individual stood behind it. "You boys come far?" he asked them. "From Arizona and across the Mesa Verde," Brian replied. The man raised his eyebrows and said, "That's dangerous country! See any Indians?" So Brian told him of the Utes they had seen. "I figured they weren't familiar with repeating rifles because they were took by surprise." The barkeep nodded and said, "Yeah, when the war was on, this part of the country was mainly left alone. Now, with the talk of gold being found, people are starting to come in."

Mark asked him, "How many in this town?" The barkeep scratched his beard and said, "Around thirty, I would say, but at any given time there will always be around fifteen men here to defend the place if the Indians attack. The rest go out prospecting for a week, and when they return the others will go out to prospect. Kind of an arrangement we made considering the situation." Brian asked him, "You folks been here long?" The barkeep shook his head and told him, "We found this place with some log buildings put up, and we added to it to kind of make a fort. I guess the people who built some of these here buildings are either long gone, or the Indians killed them."

"Any Indian attacks so far?" Mark asked. The barkeep said, "Three attacks in two months before this, but we all have Winchesters or Henry rifles, and we have a lot of ammunition, so we made them pay dearly for those attacks. Hasn't been an attack now for more than a month." He picked up a bottle and said, "Homemade whiskey, but it's good." He poured them a shot each and then asked, "You boys hunting gold?" Brian shrugged and replied, "That's the idea, but we figure on moving further north towards the San Juan mountains."

The barkeep said, "Name's Bill Riley, and I'm a man who is always looking over the horizon, which is how I ended up here. I usually do my bit of prospecting, but here I decided to open this saloon as I make a fine brand of whiskey." He paused and then said, "Besides, the ones who go out haven't found any gold up to now, and I've been figuring on moving on soon." Mark just said, "The whiskey is good, kind of like bourbon if you ask me." Bill Riley rested his forearms on the bar and said, "There's a place they're calling Silver City near the San Juan mountains where they found silver, but I heard tell from a feller that passed this way a month back that they've now found gold there or somewhere nearby most likely." He looked at Brian and continued, "Thing I'm saying is, if you boys are headed that way, you mind if I come along? We'd have three rifles instead of two, seeing that all this country right up to the San Juans is Ute country."

Brian looked at Mark, and at his nod, he told Riley, "Always good to have another gun in Indian country, but we'll be going further along the Animas river to where the west fork joins the north fork." Riley gave him a curious look and then asked, "You boys been over this trail before?" Brian shrugged and said, "Nope, but that's the direction that an old prospector, Tally Stevens, told us to head for, and so that's where we're going."

Bill Riley stood up straight and exclaimed, "Tally? You boys met up with him? Last I heard, he was headed for Arizona, but if anyone knows this country, it'd be old Tally as he's been over it since long before the Civil War started!" Brian asked him, "You know Tally?" Riley laughed and told him, "I should smile I do! I learnt my prospecting from him! My Pa and me were with him when my Pa was killed in an Indian attack. He was Tally's partner in prospecting, and that was the first trip he had taken me along because my Ma had died, and I was just itching to leave our farm and see the world! We were together for about four years, I would say, in the late forties. I was a youngster, mind you, and Tally taught me all I know about prospecting and living off the land." He paused and then asked Brian, "Where did you meet up with him?" Brian told him, "Over in Arizona, where he found his gold mine; he and three other prospectors. They were in trouble with a claim jumper who brought in a lot of hired guns, and so we kind of helped him out."

Bill Riley looked interested and asked, "Was one of his part-ners a long-legged thin individual goes by the name of Rack Jones?" Mark said, "Why yes! He's still alive, although the other two partners are dead, killed by this here claim jumper." Bill Riley told them, "My Pa gave him that name because of his lean frame. His real name is Walton Jones!" Brian said, "We figured to rest up today and start out first thing tomorrow morning. If you're coming along with us, then I suggest you pack your outfit."

That evening, the prospecting party rode in, and a meeting was held in one of the big tents. A miner with shaggy hair and a full beard with a broad face spoke first, and it was clear to Brian that he was one of the leaders. "We found traces of gold about five miles from here," he said. A cheer went up from the crowd, and he held up his hand for silence. "We found the traces in a stream, and we followed it uphill and found some deposits, but I'm sure that the main seam is still further uphill." A man in the crowd asked him, "So why did you come in, Spence, without finding it?" Spence, the man with the shaggy hair, said, "Because, Ricky, we came upon an encampment of Utes just right above where we found the deposits! Luckily they didn't see us, and we sneaked out of there without them knowing." He paused for effect and then said, "But get this, they're going to find our tracks, and they're going to watch that place, so no way are we going to take out that gold!"

There was cursing from many of the men, and one of them said, "Let's just chuck it in and go further up north. Those men who came in last time mentioned about gold being found in the San Juan mountains, so I say we go there instead of wasting our time here." Spence pulled at his beard and said, "But the San Juan is also Ute territory!" Bill Riley spoke up, "Yeah, but they also said that there was a settlement of sorts there that they are calling Silver City because they found silver there first." Spence said, "We have a settlement here, and there are about thirty of us, so what's the difference between our settlement and this here Silver City?" Brian spoke up and said, "This here discussion has nothing to do with me as I'm just passing through, but it seems to me that if you add your thirty guns to whatever guns are up there now, then you have a force that can tame those Indians." Ricky jumped up and exclaimed, "There you are, that's what I'm saying! Let's pack it in and go up north!" Spence looked at Brian and asked him, "You're going up there?" Brian shrugged and replied, "Yeah, but we're actually going further. I was just commenting on the fact that with a large enough force, you can mine gold and defend yourself from a Ute attack." Spence looked at the crowd and said, "All those in favor of going up north just raise your hands." Most of the men raised their hands, and Spence said, "Okay, those of you who didn't raise your hands, would you stand up?" Ten men stood up and one of them said, "I speak for myself, but I'm going to Arizona. There are Indians there as well, but there are enough people settled there now so that a man can mine his gold without the constant fear of an Indian attack!" Another man said, "I'm going with him!" The rest of them said the same thing, and Ricky told them, "We all made a deal to protect each other when we came here, so I'm asking you if you think that ten men are enough to make it through to Arizona or if you want us to come leave you there first before going up north." The man who had first spoken said, "Thanks, Ricky, you're a good man, but ten of us can make it through easily." Another of the men said, "And if we can't, then having another twenty men along sure won't make no difference. You boys go ahead up north, and I wish you luck, but tomorrow we are going to head for Arizona." The discussion became general, and Ricky came up to Brian and Mark, who were standing with Bill Riley. Bill introduced them, "Brian, Mark, this here is Ricky Brown, and he's been all over this country. Ricky, these are the Bailey brothers."

"You're coming with us, Bill?" Ricky asked him. Riley said, "Sure, but I'll be going further on with Brian and Mark here. They're friends of old Tally Stevens and they're going to a place that he told them to head for." Ricky said, "Well, if Tally said to head there, then I guess you should head there." Mark asked him, "You know Tally?" Ricky shook his head and explained, "I don't know Tally like Bill here does, but I know *of* him. Hell, every miner in this part of the country knows of Tally Stevens. The man's a legend in the prospecting field!" He turned and called out, "Hey Spence, come over here, will you!" Spence came over and Ricky said, "Brian and Mark Bailey meet Spence Harding. He's the man who actually started this settlement!" He told Spence, "We were talking about Tally Stevens, so tell them that tale of the gold mine in Nebraska!" Spence smiled and told them, "Tally made a gold find in a remote area of Nebraska about ten or twelve years ago. Now, on his way there, he had come upon a small settlement of around twenty five people. They were eight families, all related, and making a tough job of it to survive. They were new to the west, and they were struggling to adapt, so Tally killed some meat for them before moving on. Now when Tally found that gold, it was about forty miles from where he had seen those people, and so he turned around and went back. He told them that he would teach them to mine the gold and to hunt for their food and that by the time they had the gold out of the ground, they would be well adapted to living in the west." He paused, but no one spoke, and he continued, "After about three or four months, they had taken out all the gold there was, and they had learnt a bit about survival in the wilderness. You see, the gold was just a pocket, and it played out." He paused again, and Mark asked him, "So he shared the gold with them and then went on his way?" Spence smiled and told him, "That's the thing, he didn't share it with them...he gave it all to them and saw them to the nearest town and left them only after they had banked the gold!"

Bill Riley said, "Well, that's Tally Stevens all right! You never can say what that man will do." Spence said, "I met a man from one of those families, and he told me the tale. He said that Tally told them, 'There are twenty five of you, and you did all the work, so you divvy it up amongst yourselves.' They said that wasn't fair, as he was the one who not only found the gold but taught them all that they knew. To which he replied, 'I can always find some more. You folks need this more than I do!' That's Tally for you." Ricky told him, "Reason we're talking about Tally is because these boys are going someplace that Tally told them to go to. They're friends of his." Spence turned to Brian and said, "It's your choice, of course, and if you say no, I'd totally understand, but if Tally told you of a place, then I would be much obliged if you'd let me and Ricky come along." Brian said, "From what I hear, that place is still crawling with Utes, unlike the country around Silver City. But having said that, you're most welcome to join us, and in fact, anyone else who wants to come along as well." Ricky exclaimed, "That's mighty decent of you to be willing to share!" Brian shrugged and told him, "We don't know that there is gold there. I believe Tally when he says there is, but we don't know the difficulties we will face in taking the gold out of the ground. So whoever is willing to take the risk should have a share in the gold as well!" The next morning Ricky told Brian that, besides Spence, there were two more good miners who were willing to come along with them. "We'll all travel to Silver City, and then we seven will go on from there," he told Brian, to which Brian agreed.

They set out the next morning after meeting the two miners who were to travel with them after Silver City. The miners were Joe Lamprey and Dewey Long. Joe was a lean, tall individual with a long, mournful face, and he had a low-slung, tied-down six-gun. "Where you from, Joe?" Brian asked him. "I'm from Tennessee," he said in a low, sad voice. "It's just my luck to meet up with two of the Bailey clan, and now for sure there's gonna be a lot of shooting, and some of them bullets will be aimed at me!" Ricky laughed and said, "You can see why they call him Happy Joe! But don't be fooled, because come fighting time, Joe is always in the thick of it!" Mark smiled and asked him, "You know of the Baileys, Joe?" Happy Joe hung his head and said in his sorrowful voice, "Everyone in Tennessee knows about the feuding Bailey clan, and now I'm stuck with two of them!" Mark laughed and told him, "Don't worry, Joe, when the fighting starts, we'll just follow your lead!"

Dewey Long was a short, barrel-chested individual with bulging muscles, who seemed to have a permanent smile on his face. "I'm from Kentucky," he said. "This here happy man has been my saddle partner for a long time now. When it comes to gunplay, I take a backseat to Joe, but when it comes time for the fist and boot, then I take the lead!"

The men who had chosen to go to Silver City escorted the remaining ten miners up to the border of Arizona, and then they turned around for the journey to Silver City. They were twenty two seasoned men, all armed with repeating rifles and six-guns, and they knew how to travel in hostile country. They were too strong a force for any small roving band of Indians, and they made it to Silver City without incident. A man from the east might have laughed at the term 'city' being used to describe the log cabins and wooden framework buildings that lined the one dusty street of the settlement, but for a frontiersman, it was a large settlement and the term would not have surprised him. It was indeed quite a large settlement for the place and the time, and there were also dugouts in the hillsides and sod houses built against the hill. The dugouts and the sod houses faced the town buildings from where riflemen could cover the slopes of the hill behind them.

The town had its buildings built close together with only small gaps between, through which only one horse could pass at a time. All the buildings had windows at the back and the front with loopholes in the walls that would allow the defenders to shoot at any attacking force. The street was open at both ends, because if any raiding band of Indian warriors rode down that street, they would be cut to ribbons in the crossfire from both sides of the street.

Brian was a veteran of the Civil War and a veteran of many a battle with Indians, and he looked at the town and liked what he saw. "Smart men built this place," he said. "It would take a mighty large force of Indians to even try and take this town!" Mark said, "Maybe that's the reason why the Utes leave them alone. They must have attacked in the beginning, and they learnt their lesson."

They all trooped into the nearest saloon, which was aptly named the Silverline Saloon, and after ordering drinks, they talked with the barkeep. They found out that the population of the town was more than a hundred, which was why the Utes gave up trying to attack them. "They haven't given up trying to attack the mines," the barkeep told them. "But each mining party is made up of at least fifteen men, and they are always on guard while mining. Your group is strong enough to form your own mining partnership." He paused to give effect to what he had to say next, "Just remember that in this country, at this time, with the Utes on the warpath, there is no such thing as individual mining. Every mine is a partnership so that there are enough guns to defend it from the Utes."

Brian, Mark and the other five said their goodbyes the next morning and started out to follow the Animas River. They had ten spare horses with them, five pack mules, and a small but sturdy wagon drawn by two more mules. The mules and the wagon were loaded with supplies and ammunition.

CHAPTER 9
THE ANIMAS FORKS

IT WAS A WILD AND BEAUTIFUL LAND WITH RAVINES running through steep hillsides covered with spruce and pine trees. They rode in the direction of the Animas River, and when they reached it, they continued on a parallel course some distance away. "Best not to ride along the river as it would leave us exposed," Spence said. Ricky warned them, "We are now deep in Ute country, so stay alert!" They rode into a large, lush green valley that opened out into a huge expanse of grassland dotted here and there with pine and cottonwood groves. Brian told Mark, "This would be the perfect place for a ranch!" Happy Joe moaned, "The Utes would most likely have your hair within weeks. I just know that if you start a ranch here you're going to hire me, and I'll be a target for those Ute arrows!" Dewey Long laughed and declared, "That's the most original way of asking for a job that I've ever heard of!" Mark smiled and asked Dewey, "If we do start a ranch here, would you be interested in riding for us?" Happy Joe cried out, "There you go! Of course he would be willing, and being his saddle partner I'd have to stay too!"

They camped that evening near a creek under a stand of lodgepole pines after building a rampart made of rocks and deadfalls to provide cover in case of a Ute attack. While Bill Riley was broiling some steaks from an elk that Mark had shot that day, Joe told Brian, "I heard about the Cedar Creek battle. You boys joined forces with the Double M and your name is being spoken about along the trails." Dewey Long said, "Yeah, they're calling you the sharpshooter Baileys. The word is that you boys prefer rifles and you're deadly accurate in your shooting!" Joe shrugged and retorted, "Any boy from the Tennessee hills can bark a squirrel at the age of eight. I was more interested in hearing about two of the Baileys who are said to be fast on the draw. That would be you two?" Brian told him, "We do what we have to do when it has to be done. Anyway, Mark here is faster than I am. In fact, I've never seen anyone faster except for Jack Donovan." Dewey asked Mark, "That's the one they call Lightning Hands?" Mark smiled and told him, "He's lightning all right! He taught me a technique that has actually made me faster on the draw." Bill Riley chimed in and said, "They're hunting for gold to get a stake to start their own ranch." Brian said wistfully, "If we do, then this is the place I'd choose. We could drive in a herd from New Mexico with enough hands to hold off the Utes." Mark told him, "First let's get that gold and then we can plan on the ranch. But I'm with you on starting a ranch right here. Those mountains sure do make this a beautiful place!"

Before break of dawn, Brian awoke, but he lay still while he tried to figure out what had awakened him. He heard nothing, but his sense of danger was tingling, and he was alert. Slowly, he rolled out of his blankets and found that Mark was watching him. He signaled to Mark to get up and put his finger to his lips for silence. Putting on his hat and his boots, he crawled to the roughly built rampart that was facing uphill and squatted there with his rifle held ready. He turned around when Mark joined him and found that the others were also awake and moving to cover with their rifles. Brian whispered, "Bill, you watch the down slope using the wagon for cover. Ricky and Spence, you cover one side, and Joe and Dewey can cover the other." Joe whispered back, "You hear something?" Brian replied, "Not now, but something woke me up and I sense danger." Mark told the others, "My older brother Mike always said that it was Brian's sense of danger approaching that got them through the war, so I'd be alert if I were you!" Suddenly Brian moved back and bunched up his blankets, so that to anyone looking from a distance, it would seem like a man was sleeping there. The others caught on to the idea and quickly did the same before moving back to their positions. Brian whispered, "Absolute silence while we wait! I'm hoping that those shapes on the ground will fool them and they'll come in, so don't fire until they're close and make every shot count." They waited in tense silence, and it was Joe who first spotted the Indians. "Here they come," he whispered. One by one, the others said, "I see them also." Brian whispered back, "Wait until they're at least twenty feet away before opening fire."

The Ute raiding party had spotted them in the evening and had followed them. When the seven men had camped for the night, the Utes had spread out and waited through the night to attack in the early hour before dawn. They saw the figures rolled up in their blankets, and they advanced cautiously and silently, hoping to count coup on a live enemy. Joe whispered, "They're twenty feet away now!" Brian asked, "Anyone else see them at twenty feet away?" All except Bill Riley answered in the affirmative, and Bill said, "My group is at least forty feet away." Brian said, "Okay, everyone except Bill open fire. Bill, you wait for them to come up." Suddenly, the night was split with the thunder of repeating rifles and Indians were dropping all around the camp. The Indians in front of Bill Riley hesitated, but as there was no gunfire from that front, they must have figured that the white men were not guarding the lower slope of the hill, and they advanced rapidly up the hill. There were seven

Utes, and Bill waited until they were just fifteen feet away before he started firing, working the lever in a rapid action so that the firing seemed to be one long roll of sound. Four Indians fell to the ground, wounded or dead, and the rest managed to get away. Brian shouted out, and it was the soldier in him that demanded, "Report! How many on your side did you drop, and how many got away!" Ricky reported, "We got four, and I think five got away." Joe from the other side said, "I figure just two made it away from this side." Bill Riley said, "I got four, and three got away."

"Spence, Bill, Joe, stay where you are," Brian ordered. "Ricky and Dewey, start packing and do it fast! Mark, you help them to pack; we're leaving out of here right now!" Within five minutes, they were packed and mounted, and Brian led the way up the hill. He and Mark had accounted for all the Indians that they had seen, and so Brian chose to take that direction. But as he told the others, "We got them all, but with Indians you can never be sure, so stay alert, and if you see a dead Indian lying on the ground, just put a bullet in his head to make sure that he's dead!" They topped the hill and then rode fast for the next five miles before once again cutting across to get on the same course as the river.

Before cutting across the country, Brian had called a halt in an area that had a hard and stony surface. Getting down from his mount, he took out a burlap sack from his saddlebags and began cutting strips from it. Mark was already doing the same, and Brian told the others, "Cut strips and tie them around your horse's hooves and the mules too!" They then unloaded the wagon and distributed the load among the spare horses and the two mules that drew the wagon. Brian and Mark took out long strips of sacking that they had packed in the wagon and they carefully wrapped these around the wagon wheels. The wagon was light with its load removed, and with the padding of the sacking strips, it left hardly any track when it rolled. Spence said, "You boys came prepared for this? I wondered at the extra sacking that you packed." Brian took a moment to explain and said, "When we started out from Tennessee, we met an old mountain man on the way and he gave us this idea to conceal the wagon tracks if ever we had to run from Indians." He paused and then said, "We used it quite a bit on our trek to Kansas." When they were done, they mounted up and cut across country to get to the direction of the river, but now Brian led them at a slower pace. "The sacking on the hooves won't leave much in the way of tracks for the Utes to follow, same as with the wagon," he explained to them. "Just try and make sure that you don't disturb anything on the ground as you ride. That's why we're riding at a slower pace." After a while, he said, "They will eventually figure it out and then they'll really look, and they'll find some sign and follow us, but it will buy us enough time to get away from this raiding party." Mark commented, "They might also think that their medicine is bad and give up the chase. I figure they lost a lot of men in that attack, dead or wounded, and Indians in general don't like losing their warriors!"

They continued to climb higher as they were entering the San Juan range and the weather turned colder, but they saw no more Utes. As Mark remarked, "Maybe they think we have devil guns. I believe they're not that familiar with repeating rifles, and we have the Winchester 66. Brian can fire fifteen shots in as many seconds, and I'm a tad slower!"Joe said, "Well, my trusty Henry can still fire fifteen in just about double that time!" Spence Harding cautioned them, "Sure we have the firepower, but that's only if we don't get ambushed!" Mark agreed and added, "You should worry when you see an Indian, but you should worry more when you don't see one!" After two days of riding, with Spence leading the way as he had crossed this country before, they rode down to the river, and Spence said, "Well, there she is, the Animas Forks! That's the West Fork and this here is the North Fork." It was a rugged land with hills all around, but the area for a good distance from the river was quite level until you hit the hills. Brian said, "We must be at more than 10,000 feet altitude." Spence agreed and said, "The winters are hard here, but as this is summer, we should be fine." Happy Joe moaned, "You call this summer? I'm already starting to freeze!" Dewey consoled him, "Don't worry, Joe, once you start digging for that gold, you'll be warm enough!" They all laughed, for by now they knew that Joe's pessimism and moaning was all an act and what he really yearned for was action and danger.

Brian took charge and said, "Before we start prospecting for gold, let's build our base right here and make sure we can repel an Indian attack when it comes." They chose a spot where there was a spring that had formed a small lake, and they built near it. There was an abundance of lodgepole pines and firs on the hillsides, and they divided themselves into units. Joe and Spence were the best men with an axe, and so they took on the job of selecting and cutting down the trees for building. Dewey Long and Ricky built a stone boat to haul the cut logs down to the valley where they intended to build their town. Brian, Mark, and Bill Riley took charge of the building, and Brian soon learnt that Bill Riley was an expert in throwing up a solidly built house in the fastest time he had ever seen. Bill Riley was a good carpenter, and he even made the furniture for the buildings. Brian commented on his skill, and Bill said, "Wherever I go, I build my own house or saloon, depending on what the situation is, and over the years I guess I figured out the easiest way to get the job done. I always make my own furniture as well. I find it relaxing when I'm working with wood."

They put up four long low buildings to form a large rectangle, and they filled in two of the gaps between the buildings, which were diagonally opposite to each other, with boulders and deadfalls, leaving only two diagonally opposite exits. One of the exits had a barrier of long wooden stakes sharpened to a point and facing outwards, which would make it extremely difficult to climb over from the outside. It looked like the stakes had been planted in the ground, but in fact, all the stakes were fixed to a large wooden board. It had been cleverly designed by Bill Riley so that the entire barrier could be swung open on a pivot. Bill Riley told the others, "It was Brian's idea, and we use it only if we decide to escape from here during an attack." Brian explained his plan, "If we find ourselves trapped with no way to hold out, then we can use this exit. Since it looks impassable, the attackers won't be watching this point, and we can make our escape." In the center of the rectangle, they built their main defensive building, and that was built of stone and sod so that it could not be set on fire. Brian told them, "In case of an attack, we man the four outer buildings and fight from there. In the event we are overrun, then we fall back to this stone building. We've built an earthen cellar under it, and we intend to keep it stocked with meat and supplies at all times." Bill Riley said with a feeling of satisfaction, "I figure we could hold out for three months easy in that there building." They also dug a deep trench from the small lake so that the water ran right into the rectangle to end up next to the stone building.

It took them five months of brutal hard work from dawn to dusk to complete the small settlement, and then with winter approaching, they began to hunt meat and smoke it before storing it in the cellar. They placed all their canned food also in the cellar because it was a real cold place even before winter set in, and Brian figured the food would stay longer without spoiling. They took turns in cutting the long grass from the valley and stacked it in bales in a lean-to shed they built for that purpose. Just behind the stone building, they built a large barn to keep the horses and mules. Such was Bill Riley's skill that none of the buildings had any chinks, and they were snug and warm. All the buildings, excepting the barn, had a stone fireplace with a stone chimney for the smoke to exit. Once everything was completed, Brian had everyone working together to pitch mud and sod onto the roofs of the buildings. "It helps to keep in the warmth," he told them. "Besides, during an Indian attack, they won't be able to set it afire by shooting flaming arrows at it." While hunting for meat, they had done so far away from the settlement, again on Brian's advice. "During the winter, we might have to hunt again, and so we don't want to drive the animals away from here now," he said.

The days grew colder, and one morning they awoke to find their world wrapped in a blanket of white. Winter had set in, but they were ready, and that evening Bill Riley broke open a bottle of whiskey. "Here's to prospecting in the spring!" he said, raising a toast. "Maybe one of us should have been spared to do some prospecting these past few months," Ricky Brown commented. "Even if we didn't find gold, at least we could have found some likely places to start looking in the spring. That way, we might have been able to start mining that gold come spring or summer." Brian smiled and said, "Oh, we know where to start looking, so that's what we will be doing as soon as winter is over." Spence Harding asked him, "Tally actually told you where to look?" Brian nodded and said, "From this point, we go north-northeast, until we see a tall sentinel rock formation with the mountains in the background." Spence said doubtfully, "There are a lot of sentinel rocks around these parts, Brian." But Brian smiled again and told him, "Tally said to look for a four-foot-tall cross cut into the rock. He said he had cut it deep enough so that it would be visible for a long, long time." Spence jumped up and exclaimed, "That means he found gold! That is the only man I have ever known who could find gold and then just leave it there for later! That's the way he always marks his finds." Brian laughed and said, "He told me that for him it was always about the search and not about the finding of the gold that was in his blood." Spence grinned and said, "That's Tally for sure!"

Turning serious again, Brian continued, "Facing that mark, we turn at right angles to it and travel in a straight line until we hit a low range of hills. There we'll find his mark again." Happy Joe forgot about being sad and told Brian, "Well, let me say that I never met a man who so easily shared the location of where to find gold!" Brian shrugged and replied, "This is a wild and savage land, and anything can happen to a man out there. There are a thousand ways a man can die here, and an Indian arrow is just one of them! I'm sharing because if anything were to happen to me, then you men should know where to look." Spence gave Brian a thoughtful look and said, "Joe is right, no one would share that knowledge. But then again, ole Tally has never shared his finds with anyone, so you're the exception, and I guess that makes you special!" Brian looked uncomfortable and just shrugged, but Spence persisted and said, "You must have done something real special for Tally to give you one of his finds. There's a good story there I figure!" Finally, it was Mark who told them about Arizona and Josh Williams, and Spence exclaimed, "No wonder Tally gave you one of his finds! You saved him and his partner!"

At more than 10,000 feet, the winter did not creep in but crashed in on them, and for a week it was so bitterly cold that they only went out to feed and water the horses and mules, and to break the ice over the trench to get at the water. Bill Riley had made watertight barrels to store water, and there were two placed in each building to hold water, but even here ice formed on the top at night which had to be broken through every morning. They took turns to do these chores every day, and they split themselves into two groups, one group each to the two buildings that formed the shorter length of the rectangle. The two groups lived and slept in those buildings so that the approaches to their settlement were under constant watch. Spence Harding, Bill Riley, and Ricky Brown were in one of the buildings, while

Brian, Mark, Dewey Long, and Joe Lamprey took the other building.

After ten days of sheltering from the first cold of winter, Brian and Mark took turns with Joe and Dewey to take a ride every morning to survey the country around them and to hunt for meat. They knew that as the winter progressed, finding game would become more and more difficult, and so these daily sorties helped to keep their cellar larder supplied. It also helped them to familiarize themselves with the layout of the land. Each day, the pair that went out would take a new route, and when they came back, they would share their findings with the entire group. Brian and Mark followed Tally's directions and found the place marked with his sign. They described the trail to the others, and Brian said, "I'll take Spence with me tomorrow to see the place, as he's the expert and can tell us just how promising it looks. I figure in another two months or so we'll see the beginning of spring, and we can make a start at the prospecting." Within a month of winter setting in, they found that it was difficult to take the horses out daily for any great distance as the snow lay heavily on the ground, and it had filled in all the hollows and dips so that the land looked level, but a horse could easily lose its footing and fall and maybe break a leg or fall on its rider. Bill Riley had fashioned snow shoes from carefully selected pine boughs before the winter had set in, and these were now used to walk across the snow-laden landscape. As Mark told Bill, "You're to be complimented, Bill! These shoes make walking across the snow so much less strenuous, and we actually went as far as twelve miles today, I think!" Brian said, "Since we have been riding the trails out of here daily, they are well marked, and we take the horses as far as possible and then we hitch them to a tree and walk the rest of the way on these here snow shoes."

After three months the spring finally arrived, and they made their preparations for prospecting. Brian laid out a plan for them. "Spence and Ricky will do the prospecting, with Mark riding shotgun. The three of you will take two loaded Winchesters each with enough ammunition to start a small war! Dewey and Bill will hold the fort here, while Joe and I will scout the countryside for any signs of Indians. In case of an Indian attack on any group, the warning signal will be three fast-paced rifle shots. The sound will carry far in this place, and the other group will ride to help out." He paused and then added, "That don't apply to Dewey and Bill. You men are not to leave the settlement, no matter what you hear. If *you* fire the warning shots, then Mark, Joe, and I will come running. If we are in trouble, only Mark is to come to our aid; and if they are in trouble, then Joe and I will go to help them." Spence asked him, "Why only Mark?"

"Because you and Ricky will have to hold the mine until the trouble is over," Brian told him. "Once we start mining, we don't want to leave the place without a guard, as we might find a surprise party waiting for us on our return!" Bill Riley remarked, "It's obvious you've been a soldier, and more than that, you must have been an officer. You plan well and take care of all the details." Mark said, "He was a lieutenant in the Civil War, and our brother Mike made captain. They fought for the Confederacy." Brian shrugged and commented, "We were always outnumbered and outgunned, and so we learnt how to plan and make do with what we had available."

CHAPTER 10
GOLD RUSH

IT TOOK THEM FOUR DAYS TO LOCATE THE DIG THAT Tally had made, and they found the gold, which was a seam. But instead of starting to take out the gold immediately, Spence and Ricky did some more prospecting and found another seam further on up the hill. They then staked out both the claims, and leaving only Dewey and Joe to guard the settlement, the rest of them set to and built two cabins at each of the claims and made fortifications to defend themselves from an attack. That took another two weeks of hard labor and only when Brian was satisfied did they start to take out the gold. Leaving Spence and Ricky at the claim with Mark riding shotgun, Brian and Bill Riley rode back to the settlement. They rode to the barn to stable their horses and Bill remarked on the silence. "Wonder where Joe and Dewey are at," he said. Brian told him softly, "Just keep riding to the barn and stay sharp!"

Brian swung down from the saddle just outside the barn doors, which were open as usual, but he kept his horse between him and the barn. Bill had been watching him and now he did the same. They walked the horses into the barn instead of riding right in as they usually did. Brian stayed by the right side of his horse as he walked it into the barn, and he kept his right hand free. Without seeming to, he was scanning the barn as he walked, and a movement by one of the stalls brought him to an abrupt stop. Three men stepped out of the stall with rifles in their hands, and the man who was slightly ahead of the others said, "Hold it right there and raise your hands sky high!"

The three men made three grave mistakes when they stepped out of the stall. They expected to be facing the two riders leading their horses into the barn, which was their first mistake. Because of Brian's alertness, he was standing on the off side of his horse and his right hand was free, while Bill's horse was to his right and slightly behind him, with Bill also standing on the off side of his horse. The three men were facing Brian, but they could only see Bill's head and shoulders over his saddle. The three men had stepped out with their rifles in their hands, but the barrels were pointing to the ground, which was their second mistake. They tried to rectify their mistakes by tilting up their rifles, and one man started to move to the side to get a better view of Bill Riley, which was their third and last mistake that day. As they started their moves, Brian palmed his gun and began shooting. Bill had already drawn his gun when he entered the barn, and when Brian started to shoot, he laid his gun across his saddle and opened fire. Brian shot the two men in front of him while Bill took out the man who had started to move to the side. Three seconds after Brian's hand had dipped for his gun, the three intruders lay dead on the floor of the barn.

Three shots sounded from the building behind the barn and Brian and Bill ran towards it.

There were two more strangers in that building holding Joe and Dewey at gunpoint when the shooting started in the barn. The two strangers made the mistake of involuntarily looking backwards at the sound of the shooting. It was just for a second, but it was enough for Joe, who palmed his gun and shot them both. One of the strangers got off a shot, but it went into the ground as he started to fall with a bullet in his chest. Joe was reloading his pistol when Brian and Bill walked in. "What the hell happened here, and who are these strangers?" Bill asked Joe. But it was Dewey who gave them the story.

Joe was keeping a lookout from one building while Dewey was in the opposite building keeping a watch on the trail. Dewey saw three horses approaching at a gallop, and he kept his rifle pointed at them from a window. When they came closer, he could see that only one horse was being ridden while the other two were on a lead rope and had bodies draped over the saddles. He fired a warning shot into the ground in front of the approaching horses, and the rider drew up in a flurry of dust and shouted out, "I need some help here! Ran into a Ute war party, and these two men are badly wounded!" Joe had run all the way to the building on hearing Dewey's rifle boom, and he ran into the room and looked out the window. Dewey went immediately to open the back door, but Joe told him, "Hold it, Dew, something doesn't seem right!" There were two snicks of rifles being cocked, and a voice at the back of them said, "One wrong move and you're both dead men. Try to turn around and you're both dead men. Stand still and slowly raise your hands above your head!" He then shouted out, "Come ahead, Ron, we've got them covered!" The rider and the two men who had been lying across the saddles sprinted to the window and pointed their guns at Joe and Dewey. Dewey cursed and looked at Joe, but with a slight shake of his head Joe raised his hands and Dewey did the same. One of the strangers went and opened the back door, and the three men came into the room. Joe looked around and saw that there were a total of five men: the three who had come in from the back and the two men who had sneaked up on him. The man who had shouted out to Ron now told him, "Two of the others are headed in, so you three go to that building behind me. It's a barn, and they keep their horses there, so hide in one of the stalls until those two come in and then use your rifles on them. No fancy gun play, just use your rifles!" He looked at Joe and said, "You two stand fast and don't make any sudden moves and you may get to live. My beef is with the man riding in right now and not with you!"

When Dewey had finished telling Brian what had happened, Joe said, "It's my fault. I shouldn't have left my building and run over here because that's how these two sneaked in and had us at gunpoint before I realized that something was wrong." Dewey asked him, "You stopped me from opening the door, so what made you realize that something was off?" Joe shrugged and explained, "The bodies were draped over the saddles, but they weren't tied on, and there was no blood that I could see." Brian had been looking down at one of the men, and now he said, "This here is Rod Staver, Josh Williams' right-hand man. Guess I shouldn't have let him go free back in Arizona!" Just then Staver groaned, and Brian knelt down. "Looks like he ain't dead as yet," he said and gave Staver a little shake. Staver groaned again, opened his eyes and looked up at Brian. "You'll get yours," he mumbled. "Sent a man back and he'll spread the word about you finding gold. Shiloh Dan will be coming, and you'll pay!" Brian said, "You should have used the chance I gave you and started a new life. Instead here you are now, bleeding out on this floor! Who is Shiloh Dan anyway?" Staver glared at him and struggled to get the words out, but eventually he did and he said, "You made me back down and everyone called me a yellow-belly after that, so what chance did I have? Shiloh Dan was Josh's friend, and when he hears you've found gold, he'll come running. He's the fastest gun I've ever seen, and he'll take you and your brother!" The effort to speak brought blood bubbling up through his mouth, and he choked and died right there. "Shot through the lung," Brian said. He looked at Joe, "That was fast shooting, Joe. Both of them had their guns in their hands and you still beat them!" Joe shrugged and told him, "When you opened up in the barn they glanced back, and that gave me my chance." Brian smiled and remarked, "Like I said, real fast!"

Dewey was looking thoughtful, and now he said, "So this here hombre is part of the claim jumpers who tangled with Tally Stevens. But what's he doing out here?" Brian thought about it and then replied, "The way I read this trail is that Staver was looking for revenge. We never made a secret about where we were ultimately heading, and so he must have trailed us here. Since he said that he knows about us finding the gold, then that means that he and his crew were watching us from a distance. I bet we find field glasses in their gear!" Joe told Brian, "That idea you had about us scouting the country seems a real good one right now!"

"Staver said that he sent a man back to spread the word about us finding gold," Brian said. "It figures that there will be an influx of prospectors and miners and some unsavory characters into this area right soon." He was lost in thought for a while, and the others waited for him to continue. Eventually he told them, "Bill and Dewey will head to the mine and help them to take out the gold. Tell them what has happened and say that it's my thought that we take out that gold as fast as we can." Bill protested, "But that would leave just you and Joe to man this place and do the scouting as well!" Brian shook his head, "We're not going to worry about this settlement right now. You load up enough supplies in that wagon to last for at least ten days and you take it to the mine. After ten days Joe and I will come there, and we'll bring the wagon back for more supplies." But Bill said, "I still say that that just leaves you two to do the scouting and check on this place!" Brian agreed, but explained, "We'll do the scouting and camp out for a few days, and when we come in here we'll come real slow and cautious like. We'll make out, so let's get moving! Take the extra horses and leave us just two mules."

Bill and Dewey loaded the wagon and left for the mine. Brian told Joe, "Take enough food to last us for a month and make sure to take a lot of ammunition and some guns as well. We'll take the two mules that are left here and use them as pack horses." Joe looked puzzled and asked him, "We're going to stay out there for a month?" But all Brian said was, "You'll see. Now let's get moving!" They swiftly packed the supplies and loaded the mules, and then rode out of the settlement. They found the field glasses with Staver's horses, and they took the horses along with them. Brian picked four spots at different places that offered good concealment, and they cached supplies which included food and ammunition at each of them. They left the extra horses in a small dead-end canyon that had a stream of water and good spring grass, and they fenced the entrance so that it made a natural corral for the horses. When they were done, Brian told Joe, "Just in case the settlement gets taken over, we'll have these caches here for all of us in an emergency. It's a great thing to have handy, especially if we all get involved in a running fight with men looking to take our gold." Joe gave him a long stare and said, "You must have really been a good officer in the war! You never seem to miss a bet!" Brian smiled and told him, "It wasn't just the war, Joe. We Baileys have been fighting since I was about knee high to a grasshopper!" He shrugged and added, "Guess it's in our blood. My Pa used to tell us, if you're going to shoot, don't wait until the sun sets. So I guess we grew up being ready for anything at any time, and when shooting time comes around, we don't waste time on talking!"

They scouted all the trails for four days running, and on the fifth day they spotted some dust in the distance. Brian trained the field glasses on the dust and soon a group of six riders came into view. He studied them for a long moment and then asked Joe, who was also looking through a pair of field glasses, "So what do you think?" Joe kept looking through the glasses and said, "Four of them look like real miners, but the other two look like gunslingers." He lowered the glasses and told Brian, "See that man wearing the flat-crowned black hat and dressed all in black and riding that big black horse?" Brian didn't bother to look but asked, "What about him?" Joe told him, "That's Shiloh Dan. That's the way I heard him described. They say he comes from Utah and that he's one of the real fast guns in the West." Brian asked him, "And what do you think?" Joe shrugged and said laconically, "I ain't never seen his graveyards, but I guess we'll soon enough find out for sure!" Brian laughed and asked him, "You sure you ain't related to us Baileys? That's exactly what my Pa would say!"

They rode out to the trail the riders were travelling on and they selected a spot with good cover and they waited there with rifles held ready. Joe was on one side of the trail, and Brian chose a spot that was opposite but further down from where Joe was. The six riders came into view riding in a bunch at a slow trot, and when the last rider had passed by Joe, Brian shouted out, "Hold it right there! There's a rifle at the back of you and one in front of you. Any sudden moves and you die!" A lean, tall man who was riding at the side of Shiloh Dan went for his gun, and Brian shot him out of his saddle. "I said no sudden moves," Brian said. "The rest of you unbuckle your gun belts and let them drop. Last man to do so dies right now!" After the shooting of the lean, tall man, no one was going to argue with Brian, and the gun belts fell to the ground. "Now dismount and line up in front of the horses," Brian said. The men swung down from their saddles and walked forward with their hands held high, but Brian said, "No need to raise your hands. If anyone feels lucky enough to pull a hideout gun, go ahead and try your luck!" No one took him up on his offer, and only the black-dressed man dropped his hands. When they were lined up Joe said, "I've got them covered from here!"

Brian came out of cover and approached the men. Standing ten feet away with his rifle in his hands, he asked them, "Where you men headed?" Shiloh Dan said, "Don't see how it's any business of yours!" Brian retorted, "Wasn't talking to you! The rest of you real miners or claim jumpers?" A broad-shouldered, stocky, dark-haired man replied, "We're miners, mister! We heard about a gold strike in these parts, and we met up with this here gent and his pard, the one you shot down, on the way and we joined up to ride together." He added in explanation, "This being Ute country and all!" Brian told him, "If you're miners, you're welcome, and we'll take you to the settlement we've built. But for now you four stand to one side, and remember that my partner still has you covered, and he's a dead shot!" The four men moved away to the side, leaving the black-dressed man standing alone. "I guess that would make you Shiloh Dan," Brian told him. "I heard you were looking for me." The man frowned and said, "I'm Shiloh Dan, but I'm sure I don't know you!"

"Me and my brother took out your friend Josh Williams over in Arizona," Brian told him. "He was a claim jumper who tried to jump the wrong claim and he met with grief." Shiloh Dan glared at him and said, "If I had my guns, this talk would turn out different!" Brian said grimly, "I gave Williams a chance to ride out, and I'm giving you the same choice. But if you don't want to take it, then pick up your gun." Shiloh Dan stared at him for a long moment and then he stepped back and slowly picked up his gun belt. Just as slowly, he stepped forward and swung it around his hips. When he had finished tying down his holster and settling his gun in it, he looked up at Brian and said, "Now what? You still got the drop on me!" For answer, Brian shifted his rifle to his left hand and held it with the barrel pointing to the ground. Shiloh Dan sneered at him, and in a blur of motion he palmed his gun and was lining it up when Brian shot him in the head. Shiloh Dan died with a hole in his forehead and the sneer still on his face! There was a dead silence after the gunshot, and then Joe said mildly, "And you said I was fast. Glad we're on the same side here."

Brian told the miners about what had happened before and then said, "You're welcome to use our settlement and do your prospecting, but I'll expect you to be a part of defending the settlement as well." The stocky man stepped forward and held out his hand. "Name's Cap Miller," he said. "The Cap is short for Captain, which I was during the war." He added, "I fought for the Union." Brian smiled and told him, "I won't hold that against you, I fought for the Confederacy! I'm Brian Bailey and that sad-looking man over there is Joe Lamprey." Miller introduced the others: a short bald-headed man named John Jones, a tall broad-shouldered well-muscled man named Tiny Holden, and a short but well-built Mexican who went by the name of José Garcia. They buried Shiloh Dan and his partner in a shallow grave and caved in rocks and mud over it so that the wild animals would not dig up the grave.

They rode into the settlement, and the four miners were astonished to see the layout. "This is a fortress!" exclaimed Cap Miller. When he saw the pivoting barrier of sharpened stakes, he said, "That's the most original idea I ever saw! So tell us what we need to do and we'll get to it right away." Brian explained the strategy and said, "So Joe and I will continue to scout the area. Two of you will need to stay here, one in each building opposite to each other. Any sign of trouble and you give the signal. The other two can go to prospecting and good luck to you." John Jones asked him, "You mind if we start our prospecting around the area where you found your gold? Chances of finding more in the same area are always very high." Cap Miller said, "If we do find gold in the same area then we would go partners with you on it since it's actually your discovery."

Brian told him, "There are seven of us, and we're equal partners in whatever we take out, so I'll tell you what we can do. You go ahead and prospect, and if you find gold near to our discovery, then you split it five ways. One share to each of you and one share for us seven, which we'll divvy up among ourselves." Tiny Holden held out his hand and said, "You're a straight shooter, and that's a mighty fine offer. Any trouble that you face from here on in, you can count on the four of us to back your play." José Garcia said with a straight face, "Yeah, that's mighty white of you!" Then, still straight-faced, he added, "That's a brown man joke." Brian laughed out loud and said, "You and Joe should get along real well!"

Brian told Joe to take Tiny and John to the mine and do the introductions, while he showed Cap and Garcia around the settlement. When Joe came back, he and Brian ate a meal and then started out again. As they were leaving, Cap told Brian, "I figure you can expect a lot more folk coming in. By the time we left, the news had already spread about a new gold mine." Brian shrugged and said, "If they're honest, they're welcome, but our offer is only for you four. The others who come can prospect on their own wherever they want."

A week later, Joe spotted a large dust cloud in the distance, and after using his field glasses, he told Brian, "There's a dozen of them this time." They rode back to the settlement, and Brian told Cap Miller, "I'm selling one of these buildings on the shorter side of the rectangle to your group right now. We'll hold onto the stone building, the other shorter-length building and the barn, and sell the remaining two longer buildings to those who want to buy them. But any new buildings are going to have to come up outside of this here rectangle because we've laid claim to this spot." They rode out again and met the men who were riding in. "Mister," one of the newcomers told Brian. "We heard about a gold strike in this area and we're here to do some prospecting. I figure you're the one who found the gold since you're here already, so is there any kind of town or something which we could use as a base?" Brian told him about the settlement, and the man said, "I'm Marvin Ridley, and we're a team and we're going to work together, so we'll buy one of those buildings right now!" The others nodded in agreement, and Brian and Joe led them back to the settlement and told them to take one of the buildings on the longer side of the rectangle. "These are bigger by design to form a rectangle," he told them. "You're a dozen men, so you could use the extra space."

Two months later, Brian and the others in his group were sitting in one of the cabins at the mine, which they had named the Tally Discovery mine. Spence was addressing the group. "We've taken out a good bit of the gold in both our claims, and I figure it should be worth more than sixty thousand dollars. That's nearly nine thousand dollars for each of us right now, and in a few more days that's going to go up a lot more as we've hit a deep rich seam." Bill Riley said, "We've taken it out of the ground, but now we've got to get it to a bank in a town. One of the newcomers told me in the bar that Wells Fargo has opened an office in Silver City now."

The strength of the settlement had gone up in two months to around a hundred, and once a week Bill Riley would tend bar in the building that they had kept. More buildings were coming up around the original settlement, some roughly put-together shacks, some carefully and snugly built wooden cabins, and even some tents. Gold had been found in quite a few places, and some more buildings and dugouts were coming up some distance away near a hillside where four claims had been staked out. Spence was talking again, and he said, "Cap and his group have taken out about fifteen thousand dollars' worth of gold from their claim, and they are also looking to get it to Silver City." Riley told Brian, "That second group of twelve made a good strike and they work like demons! They say they've already taken out about thirty thousand dollars' worth of gold, and they are nervous about keeping it at the mine." Brian stayed silent and finally Mark told him, "They want us to take the gold to Silver City and deposit it with Wells Fargo." Brian said seriously, "That's more than a hundred thousand dollars in gold! If word of this gets out, then all the claim jumpers and outlaws in five states will be waiting to ambush us on the trail!" Mark agreed and said, "That's why I figure this should be done immediately before the word spreads!"

Brian told Spence, "Taking our gold and Cap Miller's gold I understand, but Ridley's gold? What makes them think they can trust us not to run off with their gold?" It was Joe who answered and said, "Turns out Marvin Ridley's mother is a Lamprey, and he says that if he can't trust a Lamprey, then he can't trust anyone!" Brian smiled and told him, "Good to know that you're volunteering to come with us on this dangerous trip!" Joe immediately put on a doleful face and said, "I always have bad luck, but what choice do I have? Can't send you and Mark without someone to watch your backs!" In a sorrowful tone he added, "Figure I'll most probably collect a few Ute arrows on the way, but a man can't dodge fate!" Everyone laughed, and Spence said, "We thought you, Mark, Joe, and Dewey could make the run to Silver City with the gold." Riley said, "Hell, if anyone can make it through, it'd be you four!" Brian thought about it, and after a while he said, "We have the wagon and the mules right here, so we can load up our gold. Cap and Marvin can load their gold on mules or horses and bring them here to load in the wagon without saying anything to anyone. They should act as though they were just taking a ride to visit us. We'll leave in three days!"

Brian and his team sat down with Spence after the gold had been loaded in the wagon. "You've been through this country before this," Brian told Spence. "What I'm looking for is an alternative route to Silver City." Spence said, "Well, there aren't many trails out of here, and besides, you have a wagon. That kind of limits the possibilities." He thought for a moment and then said, "The trail we used runs almost parallel to the Animas River, and that's the trail that most everyone uses right now. But you could go west from here and turn at Hanson's Peak, and that trail will also take you to Silver City. But that's only an old Indian trail and you would need me along to guide you." Brian asked him, "But is it passable with the wagon?" Spence shrugged and told him, "The time I used it I would say it's possible. We may have to ease the wagon over some rough spots, but I'd say it's doable!" Brian made up his mind and said, "Okay, you're coming with us, and Dewey you'll be staying here." He held up his hand as Dewey started to protest and said, "We can't spare more than four men for this trip, much as I would like to have you along."

CHAPTER 11
THE RIDE TO SILVER CITY

THEY STARTED OUT IN THE MIDDLE OF THE NIGHT, with Spence driving the wagon and Brian, Mark, and Joe scouting ahead for any signs of an ambush. They crossed the usual trail that ran south and continued towards the west. From then on, Spence gave them directions and a landmark to head for, and Brian and Mark acted as advance scouts, with Joe riding shotgun alongside the wagon. When day broke, they were well on their way, and they camped by a spring for breakfast and coffee. Brian said, "Even if we left without alerting anyone, we still could be heading into an ambush." Joe asked him, "How do you figure that if no one saw us leave?" But Brian told him, "Claim jumpers and outlaws will know by now that a lot of gold has been found, and they know that at some point we're going to have to transport that gold. They could just pick a likely spot for an ambush on the trail to Silver City and wait for the gold to be transported. That's why I wanted an alternative route."

Spence was listening with a thoughtful expression on his face, and now he said, "This is a little-used trail, but there's always a chance that some outlaw knows about it. If they do, then I figure they would try to ambush us near Hanson's Peak.

There's a lot of tree cover in that area!" He took a thin stick of wood and drew a rough map in the sand. "This here is the trail that we are taking, and this is Hanson's Peak where we turn south again. Now, here and here are the most likely places for an ambush. This place here has a heavy tree cover, and the trail runs right through it. This here is a long canyon, but not too deep, so we would be exposed to anyone hiding over the lip of the slope." Brian studied the map and asked, "Can we go around the trees?" Spence thought about it and then said, "Maybe, but it would add another ten miles to our route." He paused in thought, and after a moment he said, "Yeah, I figure it can be done, but there's no way to avoid that canyon because on either side there's no trail for a wagon, only for horses." Brian shrugged, "So we detour around the forest. We'll deal with the canyon when we get there."

They took the detour around the forest and rode on until Spence drew the wagon to a halt. "Over that ridge, the land slopes down and then narrows into a canyon. There ain't any other way to take the wagon except through that canyon," he told Brian. "You know this place," Brian said. "If you were setting up an ambush, which side of the canyon would be best, or would you set up the ambush on both sides of the canyon?" Spence thought about it and then said, "Actually, the left side of the canyon is a pretty steep drop and you can't ride a horse down it, but the right side is a steep slope which you can ride down. So the ambush would have to be set up on the right side, although they may have a rifle or two on the other side as well." Brian made his decision and told him, "You stay here with the wagon and keep your rifle handy. We'll go across the hill and come up on the right side of that canyon." He rubbed his chin and said, "Don't move if you hear shooting; move only when you hear three rapid rifle shots and nothing else." Spence replied, "I hear you!"

Brian, Mark, and Joe rode up the hill on a parallel path to

where Spence said the canyon would be. The land was a rolling hill which from above would have looked like large waves on the sea. There was no trail, and there was no way that a wagon could have driven through. Even on horseback, they rode slowly, weaving their way between trees and around huge boulders and smaller rocks. Joe had been studying the ground as he rode, and he suddenly held up a hand and said, "Hey, look here, horse tracks!" They weren't really tracks, just indentations and smudges here and there, but Brian and Mark could also read sign, and they agreed with Joe. Brian told Joe, "Figure you're better than we are at reading sign, so we'll follow you, but go slowly and stop when the tracks turn off towards the canyon." Joe went forward with Brian and Mark following, and after a mile, he pulled up and pointed to where the tracks turned off towards the canyon. "From Spence's directions, I figure we must be less than a mile away from that canyon," Brian said. "We ride slowly for half that distance, and then we go the rest of the way on foot."

After about half a mile, they tied their horses to a tree, and with their rifles held ready they walked forward slowly. Brian and Mark scanned the land ahead, looking closely at every bit of cover, while Joe was looking down and following the tracks. Suddenly, Brian moved forward and tapped Joe on the shoulder. When Joe looked up, Brian pointed ahead, and just beyond the tree line he could see three men hunkered down behind a large boulder, watching the canyon beyond. Brian, Mark, and Joe moved apart and then began to advance silently, with their fingers on the triggers. When they came out of the tree line, they saw that there were a total of seven men lined up behind boulders and single trees, watching the canyon down the slope. "You boys just drop your guns and raise your hands," Brian said. "Turn around, and you're dead!" All the seven men spun around, lifting their rifles as they turned, and there was a rolling thunder of rifle shots that echoed across the hills. When the smoke cleared, they could see that all seven were on the ground. Two were cursing and struggling to rise, while the others just lay still. "Check for dead or wounded," Brian commanded as he went towards the two wounded men who were sitting up and trying to draw their pistols.

He reached down and took away their guns and asked, "Where you wounded?" One man cursed him, and the other said, "I'm hit in the chest and I can't feel my right hand." Mark and Joe came up, and Joe said, "These two are the only ones alive." Brian told him, "Watch this one; he says he's got a chest wound." He went over and roughly checked the other outlaw and found a bullet hole in his chest from which blood was slowly seeping. "I think the bullet may have hit your lung," he told the man. "Anyone on the other side of the canyon?" The man cursed him and tried to spit, but blood welled up through his mouth, and he fell back down. "Watch him," Brian told Mark as he went over to the other wounded outlaw. "Hold him down," he told Joe. While Joe held down the man, Brian began pulling off the man's boots, and the man asked him, "What the hell you doing?" Brian said mildly, "When I lived among the Apaches, I found that the most painful thing for a man to bear was having his feet set on fire." The man shouted, "You're crazy! You ain't going to do that!" Joe looked down at him and shook his head sadly. "I've always said that the time he spent with those Apaches made him more Indian than white man," he told the man in a mournful voice. The man grew desperate as he saw Brian gathering together twigs and dry leaves to start a fire, and he said, "Mister, mister…just ask me anything and I'll tell you. You don't have to burn my feet…please mister…just ask me!" Brian gave him a thoughtful look as though he was considering the matter, and then he said, "Are there any men on the other side of the canyon?" The man shook his head, "No mister, just the seven of us on this side. Baby Face Boyd told us to wait here just in case you came this way, but he was sure you wouldn't know this route, so he's waiting on the trail to Silver City with ten men." Joe said, "Baby Face, huh? He's into bushwhacking now?" The man said, "We got the word of gold being found near the Forks, and Shiloh Dan asked Baby Face to join him, but Baby Face told him to go ahead as he had other plans. Later, he told us that eventually the miners would have to ship their gold, and they would come to Silver City, so for the last five days we've been camping out here, and Baby Face is camping on the trail."

Brian asked Joe, "You know this Baby Face Boyd?" Joe shrugged and said, "Heard of him, never met up. They say he has an innocent-looking boyish face, hence the name, but he's a stone-cold killer and said to be mighty fast on the draw. He's an outlaw, and his guns are for hire, but I heard that he usually holds up stages and robs travelers, but I never heard of him being a bushwhacker." The wounded outlaw said, "He ain't no bushwhacker! He would have held you up and then given you your chance to fight or surrender. He never shoots a man in the back!" Brian said, "An outlaw with a code of honor! Well, it's not that rare in these parts, so I'll accept your word on it." Joe asked him, "What are we going to do with this one? The bullet went through his chest, and I think it didn't hit anything. He's lucky, I guess!" Brian said, "Tend to his wound, and then we'll take his boots and all the horses and leave him here." The man struggled to get up and shouted, "You might as well kill me right here! Without a horse and barefoot! No way I can survive!" Brian said mildly, "We'll leave your boots and one horse two miles back that way. We'll leave you a canteen of water as well. You'll make out, only you won't be able to ride and warn Baby Face in time before we get to Silver City."

They got the wagon through the canyon, and Spence said with a sigh, "Well, from here on the land is wide open, and if they set up an ambush we'd be able to spot it in time. I guess we have a clear run to Silver City, so our problems are over!" Brian said mildly, "I agree our problems are over." After a moment, he added, "Until we get to Silver City!" Joe looked at him, "You think he'll be waiting for us there? But that man said that Baby Face was waiting on the trail for us, so how would he be waiting in Silver City?" Brian told him, "If it was me, I'd have a man watching both the trails. Not much cover needed for a single man to stay hidden. If we were to take the straight route to Silver City, then that lookout would ride to tell the other lookout and then ride hard to meet up with Baby Face. That way, those men at the canyon would be told by their lookout that we were going the other way, and they'd hightail it for Silver City. Since we took the Hanson's Peak trail, that lookout would have ridden to warn the other lookout and then taken a fast ride to join up with the men at the canyon, which was why they were in position and waiting for us. Now that other lookout would have ridden to tell Baby Face that we took the other route, and you can bet your bottom dollar that he's waiting at Silver City to see if his men come in or we do!" Joe stared at him for a long moment and then shrugged, "I've said it before, and I'll say it again, you must have been a real good officer! You just don't miss no trick!"

The rest of the ride was without incident, and when they were nearing Silver City, Brian said, "Stay sharp! They see us and they'll come out to meet us. They won't want to take us down in the town." They were two miles away when Brian pointed out some dust in the distance and said, "Bet that's the lookout riding hard to tell Baby Face that his men at the canyon just didn't make it." They were within a mile of the town when they saw a dust cloud approaching, and Brian said, "Mark, you and Spence keep an eye to the rear. Joe and I will handle the front." Joe looked at him but said nothing except to loosen his gun in his holster. The dust cloud drew nearer, and the riders pulled up sharply when they were just twenty feet away. The dust blew away in the wind, and Brian saw four riders facing them. Joe said softly, "The one in the middle, I'd guess is Baby

Face." The man shouted out, "You men want to live, you just throw down your guns and ride away." The riders were moving slowly forward, and they halted when ten feet away. Baby Face said, "You ride away without that there wagon!" Brian never said a word, but as if on cue, he and Joe palmed their guns and opened fire. Brian's first bullet took Baby Face through his teeth, and he was thrown off his horse. Brian took out one more, and Joe took out the other two. At the same time, Mark and Spence had opened fire at three men who had come running in from the cover of some trees. Mark downed two of them before Spence's rifle boomed and took out the third one.

When the shooting ended, Brian just said, "Let's ride for the town as fast as we can!" Without checking to see if the outlaws were dead or wounded, they rode fast and only slowed down when they entered the main street of the town. They continued up the street until they spotted the Wells Fargo office and drew rein when they reached it. With Brian, Mark, and Joe watching the street with rifles held ready, Spence walked into the office. He came out with two men who helped him to unload the gold and carry it in. Brian went into the office with Spence while Mark and Joe stood in front and continued to keep a watch on the street.

Brian and Spence came out of the office, and Brian told Mark and Joe, "I've got separate receipts from Wells Fargo for the gold. Our share they'll transfer to our bank in Cedar Creek. When we set out, I got a letter from our bank authorizing us to draw money from any branch of the bank in the country. So now we have around twenty-five thousand dollars that we can draw on to start ranching." He handed a receipt to Joe and said, "This here is your share. Spence is holding the rest of the share receipts, including Miller's and Ridley's. Now let's go have a drink and celebrate!" The town had grown a lot since they had last seen it, and there were horses hitched at the front of every building. There were wagons and riders coming into town and leaving it, and every wagon had a heavy escort of armed men. "Looks like the mines are booming," Spence remarked. Mark said, "Yeah, they even have a Marshal's office now!"

They walked into the Silverline Saloon and found the same barkeep standing behind the counter. He looked at them for a moment and then nodded his head. "Welcome back, gents!" he said. "Word is that gold is being mined at the Animas Forks, so I figured that must have been you. You make out okay?" Brian said, "We've just been to the Wells Fargo office." The barkeep reached for a bottle and glasses and said, "Guess that says it all. The first one's on the house!" He poured their drinks and said, "Name's Flint McCoy." Brian introduced the others and said, "This looks like a real boom town!" Flint shrugged and remarked, "I've seen a few, seen them born and seen them die." He paused thoughtfully and then added, "But I think this one will last. They're finding more silver than gold, but that's what will keep this town going, I think."

"Looks like the town's got a Marshal now," Mark remarked. Flint just looked at him and swiped at the counter with a damp rag. Mark looked puzzled and said, "We saw the Marshal's office as we were coming over here." Flint sighed and told him, "Yeah, we have a Marshal's office, but I wouldn't call the man sitting there a town Marshal!" Brian was curious and asked him, "Just exactly what *are* you saying, Flint? The man is not fit to be a Marshal, or the man is crooked?" Flint straightened up and told them, "Recently, a lot of bad characters came into town. They didn't come to mine for gold or silver, they came to take what the miners worked for. They got some people together and held an election and put one of their friends in as Marshal. The trouble is, the business people in this town just won't stand together, and so these roughnecks are having a free run of the place!" Brian asked him, "Claim jumpers?" But Flint shook his head and said, "It ain't as simple as that. They find a claim that is paying, and then they force the miner to sign it over to them.

Their Marshal then says that the sale is legal and the miner has no rights. They then sell the claim back to the same miner if he wants to buy it back, or they sell it to someone else!" Joe asked him, "You mean they don't bother to work the claim, they just sell it?" Flint nodded and then added, "Yeah, so the Marshal says they ain't claim jumpers, they're just regular business-men!" Brian shook his head sadly and remarked, "Always something new!" He paused for a moment and then added, "Actually, it's not something new. It's the same old claim jumping, just covered with a different skin!"

CHAPTER 12
SILVER CITY

THEY LEFT THE BAR AND HEADED FOR A HOTEL IN search of rooms for a night's sleep. They were coming up to the Marshal's office when they saw four men crowding a young girl against a wall and shouting at her. Brian walked faster and as he drew close, he heard one of the men tell the girl, "Now you get your granddaddy to sign that bill of sale or something is gonna happen to him. What will happen to you if something happens to him, huh? You get the message?" Brian stopped at the back of the men and said, "I think you men should just walk away now!" Slowly the four men turned around and a weasel-faced lanky man with dirty long hair, held down by a flat-brimmed hat, said, "My advice to you, stranger, would be to stay out of something that doesn't concern you!" He had a low-slung gun on his right thigh, and as he spoke, his hand hovered over it. Speaking casually as though he were discussing the weather, Brian asked him, "You going to draw that gun or is that just the way you usually hold your hand." The man snarled, "Mister, you're really asking for it…" His voice trailed off as he found himself staring at the gun in Brian's hand. His eyes went from the gun to Brian's face, and he licked his lips nervously. He shot a look at his companions and found them staring, but not at Brian. He looked to the side of Brian and saw Mark, Joe, and Spence standing there with their rifles in their hands. He licked his lips again and turned back to Brian. "Look, Mister," he said. "You all are strangers in this town, and you got no call to meddle in our business affairs. We ain't doin' nothing wrong here."

"I thought I heard you tell the young lady that if her grand-daddy didn't sign a bill of sale then something bad would happen to him," Brian said. "Sounds like a threat and not just business to me!" The man shot a glance again at his companions and then said, "I didn't say that." Brian stared at him grimly and asked, "You calling me a liar?" The man licked his lips again. Calling a man a liar in the West meant you had to back it up with gunplay. The girl had moved away and was standing ten feet to the side watching the scene. Brian said, "Drop your gun belts, all of you. Drop them or draw, your choice!" There were a couple of snicks of rifle hammers being drawn back, and the other three men quickly unbuckled their gun belts and let them drop. The weasel-faced looking man glared at Brian and said, "They call me Dead Shot Dillon. You want to brace me without your friends backing you up?" Brian dropped his gun in his holster and retorted, "They are just watching my back is all. You just have to worry about me because I aim to change your name." The man said, "Change my name…" As he spoke, he went for his gun, and Brian shot him dead. He told the other three men, "Take him away, and if I see you bothering this young lady again, then I'll send you to join him in Boot Hill!"

Just then the Marshal's door opened and a man with a badge came out. He looked at the man lying dead on the boardwalk and asked the three men, "What happened here?" But it was Brian who said, "Nothing much, he just drew on the wrong man. And where were you all this time when these real tough men were threatening a young lady?" The Marshal was a broad-shouldered, well-built man wearing two tied-down guns with crossed gun belts. He had a broad face with deep-set, expressionless eyes. He turned those eyes on Brian and demanded, "What's your name, stranger!"

"What's yours, Mister!" Brian retorted. "I'm the Marshal," the man said. "You either answer me or I'll run you in!" Brian said softly, "You either answer *me* or I'll run *you* out of this town." One of the men whispered urgently to the Marshal, and he looked at Mark and the others standing in the street with their rifles. "You men willing to shoot down a lawman?" he asked Mark and the others. Joe shrugged and replied, "Depends on the lawman." Brian said, "I don't think you're a duly elected Marshal. In fact, I heard that you're just an outlaw elected by outlaws." He then added, "You got a choice to make: tell me your name, or I run you out of town. I might add that I'm not a patient man!" The Marshal said, "I'm Seth Walker. Maybe you heard of me!" But it was Joe who answered him. "Yeah, I heard of you," Joe said. "A wannabe gunman who folks say is a bushwhacker and a weasel, who will only face a man if the odds are in his favor!" Seth Walker glared at Joe and said, "You wanna repeat that without holding a rifle on me?"

"Come out into the street and I will," said Joe. Walker looked at the others and Joe said, "Don't worry, no one will interfere. I don't play by *your* rules, I fight fair!" Walker stared at Joe and hesitated, and Brian said, "Yeller through and through. Either do what he says or drop your gun and the badge!" Seth Walker took a deep breath and walked out into the street. He turned to face Joe, who had handed over his rifle to Mark and was standing nonchalantly facing him. Walker's hand grabbed for his gun in a blur of motion, and Joe shot him when his gun was only halfway out of his holster. He staggered back and tried to complete his draw, and Joe shot him again, and this time the bullet found his heart and Seth Walker fell dead in the dusty street.

Flint and a couple of other businessmen were standing

across the street, and now they came forward. Flint bent and removed the badge from the body. He held it out to Brian and said, "We need a good Marshal for this town right now!" But Brian told him, "Give it to Joe and swear him in!" Joe looked at Brian in surprise and said, "You sure about this, Brian?" It was Mark who answered him. "Go ahead and take the badge, Joe," he said sadly, perfectly mimicking Joe's mournful voice. "I just know that you're going to swear me in as your deputy, and me being your friend and all, I can't refuse. I just knew something bad was going to happen when I met you!" Even Joe laughed at Mark's mimicry, and Brian said, "Let's all go into the Marshal's office and get this done. Mark, you put those three men in jail for now." He told Flint, "You get together the legit people of this town and we'll hold us an election." He walked over to the girl and said, "Miss, my name is Brian Bailey and I would like to know what they were threatening you about."

"I'm Sue Allen," the young girl told him. "I can't thank you enough for helping me out, but I'm afraid that you've bought yourself a pack of trouble!" Brian smiled at her and said, "Trouble's beginning to sound like my middle name. But tell me what was going down when I called them out." Sue Allen looked at him and liked what she saw. "My grandfather, Chet Allen, recently made a good strike in a range of hills nearby," she told him. "There are miners there who have found silver, but Grandpa found a seam of gold in a cave. He staked his claim and we've been working it, but Red Carson found out about it and he sent his men in one day and they tried to make Grandpa sign over the claim to them." Brian asked her, "Who's Red Carson?" She stared at him in surprise and said, "So you're really a stranger here! Red Carson is the leader of the gang of claim jumpers. Those men are from his crew and so was the Marshal! So you really didn't know the trouble you were walking into?" Brian shrugged and said, "I've run up against claim jumpers before. So when they braced your Grandpa, what happened?"

Sue Allen said with a small smile, "Grandpa may be old but there isn't any backup to the man! He faced them with a loaded shotgun in his hands, and he had his rifle right next to him. They backed off then, but when I came into town today to get some supplies, those men cornered me and warned me to get my Grandpa to sign that sale deed."

Sue Allen was a slim, tall young woman who couldn't have been more than twenty years of age. She had sharp features and was very good-looking, with long blond hair tied in a braid. Unusual for the time and place, she wore a shirt tucked into denim pants with moccasins on her feet. She wore a sheepskin coat that reached to her knees, but as she moved, Brian saw that she also wore a gun belt slung around her hips. "Where's your Ma and Pa?" he asked her. She shook her head and told him, "Ma died when I was about three, and Pa died three years ago in a shootout in a town in Nebraska. I have only my Grandpa and he decided to come here to find enough gold to set me up in the East. He says he isn't getting any younger, and he's worried about what would happen to me when he's no more." She paused and then added, "I told him he didn't have to worry, that I'd make out, but he won't listen." Brian asked her, "What was the shootout about? I mean the one in Nebraska." She suddenly looked sad, but she told him, "Pa was a lawman all his life. He was Marshal in that small town when a gang of outlaws rode in. He told them to ride out and they drew on him. There were three of them and he killed them all, but he took two bullets in the chest and he died of infection a month later." Brian said, "I'm sorry to hear that, but he did what a good lawman always does, and he went down fighting." He pointed to her waist and asked, "Your Pa teach you to shoot?" She smiled when she said, "He did, and he once told me that I was almost as fast as he was on the draw!"

Mark came up just then and said, "Everyone's waiting on you, Brian. They sent me to see if this young lady had maybe kidnapped you!" Sue Allen blushed and Brian said, "Don't mind him. Sue Allen, meet my younger brother Mark Bailey." Mark shook her hand solemnly and said, "Pleased to meet you, Sue Allen. Now would you mind if I dragged my brother away from you?" She smiled and said, "What makes you think that he needs to be dragged away?" Mark smiled back and told her, "It's obvious that the two of you aren't aware of the time, but you've been standing here talking for about half an hour!" Both Sue and Brian looked surprised, and this time it was Brian who turned red in the face. "Come on," he told Mark. "Let's go get this done. Sue, you're coming with us, and after we're sworn in we'll take you to your Grandpa."

They went into the Marshal's office, and when they came out, the town had a new Marshal and two deputies. Joe refused to be the Marshal, so Brian was sworn in, and he deputized Mark and Joe. Brian asked Joe, "What you told Seth Walker? You knew it wasn't true, so you were just pushing him?" Joe explained, "He was an outlaw but he was no back shooter. A while back he shot and killed a distant kin of mine, and that man was good with a gun. No, I just wanted to see how good he really was since the man he shot was my kin." He then asked Brian curiously, "What did you mean when you said that you'd change Dead Shot Dillon's name?" Brian said mildly, "I meant I'd remove his middle name." Joe thought about that and then laughed, "I get it. He's now just Dead Dillon!" They decided that Spence had to go back to Animas Forks with the gold receipts, and so he went back in the company of five miners who were headed that way to prospect for gold.

Leaving Mark and Joe to watch the town, Brian rode with Sue Allen to the gold claim. He was pleased that she didn't bother with riding sidesaddle, as was the custom for women at the time, but instead rode astride, and he noted that she was a real good rider. Chet Allen met them at the cave entrance, and he was carrying his shotgun in the crook of his arm. After the introductions, Sue told him about what had happened in town and that Brian was now the Marshal. Chet thanked Brian for helping Sue, but added, "Although she can take care of herself, four men would have been too many. Now if there were even two men, they might have been in for a surprise!" Brian said, "I noted the gun belt she wears." Chet told him, "Not just wears, she's fast on the draw and she shoots straight!" Sue protested, "Come on, Grandpa, you trying to frighten Brian away?" Chet looked at Brian thoughtfully and told her, "No child, I don't think this man frightens at all! He's been up the creek and over the mountain, I'd say." Changing the subject, Brian told him, "You stay put here with Sue, but stay on guard and never mind the gold. When this is over, we'll help you to mine the gold. Right now I got to ride back to town."

"What you figurin' on doin', Brian?" Chet asked him. Brian told him as he swung into the saddle, "I'm going to hunt some vermin." Chet said, "I heard that Red Carson hangs out in a dugout outside of town. You catch hold of a weasel-looking man who goes by the moniker of Dead Shot Dillon and he'll know where Red Carson is." Brian told him, "I'm afraid I can't do that." Chet looked surprised and asked, "Why not?" Turning his horse, Brian said over his shoulder, "He's the one I shot today."

Brian rode back to town and held a meeting with Mark and Joe at the Silverline Saloon. "Chet says that Red Carson hangs his hat in a dugout outside of town," Brian told them. "Trouble is, there's a lot of dugouts around this here town!" Mark asked Flint, "You know where he hangs his hat?" Flint shrugged and replied, "No, but there are three of his men who stay at the Rocky Mountain Hotel down the street." Brian asked him, "Where do the rest of his crew stay?"

"I wouldn't know," Flint said. "They come and go, but I'm sure they don't stay in town. These three men at the hotel front for Carson as the businessmen who buy and sell mining claims." Mark asked him, "You know their names?" Flint thought for a moment and then said, "I heard one of them being addressed as Hook. He's a tall, rugged-looking individual with a square face and a prominent hooked nose, so I guess that's why they call him Hook." Mark asked, "So what exactly do these three men do?"

"Well," said Flint. "Whenever they force a miner to sign a bill of sale, these three show up with the sale deed and claim that they bought the mine fair and square. Three weeks ago, one of the miners called Hook a liar on the street, and Hook shot him down. He told the onlookers that no man called him a liar and lived!" Brian stood up, "Well, let's go see this honest businessman!"

They walked into the bar of the Rocky Mountain Hotel and saw a man who fit the description of Hook standing at the bar with two other men. All three were dressed in range clothes, but the clothes were neat and clean, and all three wore tied-down guns. Brian stopped five feet away from the bar, and Mark and Joe spread out on either side of him, standing so that they could see the entire room and the entrance as well. "Hook!" Brian called out. The man turned slowly around and looked at Brian and the others. "I don't know you, stranger," he said. "But only my friends call me Hook!" Brian said, "These two your friends? It figures, I guess...birds of a feather!" Now all the three were facing them and Hook said, "Now what do you mean by that?" Brian gave him a level look and said, "You all look like the claim jumpers and thieving rats that you are; birds of a feather!" Hook glared at him but he was suddenly cautious. "You seem right eager to meet your maker, stranger," he said. Brian seemed to consider that and then, shaking his head, he said, "No, I don't think I'll meet my maker this time. But you will, unless you tell us where Red Carson is!" Hook said, "Don't know any Red Carson." Immediately Brian said, "You're a liar!" As he said it, he palmed his gun and the three men froze with their hands on their gun butts. "Nobody calls you a liar and lives," Brian told him. "That's what you claim, so I just called you a liar and I'm still standing here." Hook licked his lips nervously, "I don't know what you're saying, stranger. I don't know any Red Carson."

"Drop your gun belts," Brian commanded. "Do it right now or I'll shoot you in the knee, and you'll never walk straight again!" Carefully, all three of them unbuckled and dropped their belts. Brian walked up to them and again asked Hook, "Where do I find Red Carson!" Hook said, "I tell you I don't know…" Before he could complete his sentence, Brian backhanded him across his face, and he fell against the bar. Brian walked up to him and said, "I'll ask you just one last time, and then I'm going to beat you to a pulp. You're a thieving, murdering weasel who ain't fit to live."

Staring at Brian's remorseless face, Hook cringed, and when Brian raised his hand, he cried out, "Don't…don't…Red stays in a dugout out of town!" Brian slapped him and said, "I know that…tell me where this dugout is!" Hook covered his face with his hands and cried out, "I swear I don't know, but *he* does!" He was pointing at one of the other men, a short, stocky man with a mean face and small, beady eyes. Brian turned to him and the man said, "You try that with me and I'll kill you with my bare hands, gun or no gun!" Brian walked up to him and when they were a mere six inches apart, he suddenly raised his foot and stomped down on the man's kneecap with his boot. The man howled in pain and collapsed on the floor. Bending down, Brian caught hold of his shirt near the throat and effortlessly lifted him up and then dragged him across the room and threw him in a chair. Without saying a word, he stretched out the man's hand and hit his elbow hard with his gun barrel. The man howled again in pain and cried out, "You can't do this…who the hell are you!" Brian told him, "I'm a man who just does not like vermin. My Pappy always told me that when I see vermin the best thing to do is to just kill it." He paused as though in thought and then added, "See, I always listen to my Pappy, but this time I'm going to break you bone by bone until you tell me where I can find Red Carson." The casual way Brian spoke without raising his voice, and his grim face, told the man that Brian would do exactly what he said. The man looked into Brian's bleak green eyes, and he shuddered. "At the back of the Marshal's office there's just one large dugout against the hillside," he told Brian. "That's where Red will be." Brian told Mark, "Tie them up and dump them in jail. I'll be back!" Mark told Joe, "You do that, I'm going with him." Joe pulled out some rawhide strips from his pocket and quickly tied the hands and legs of the three men. Then he told the bartender, "You keep a gun on these three, and if they're not here when I come back, then I'll just naturally have to shoot you!"

He ran out of the hotel and caught up with the two brothers. "You're not leaving me out of the fun," he told Mark. "What about those men?" Mark asked him. Joe shrugged and said, "The bartender is keeping an eye on them until I get back."

CHAPTER 13
RED CARSON

They walked to their horses and swung into the saddles. Brian and Mark unsheathed their rifles, and they rode around the Marshal's office and immediately saw the large dugout about a hundred feet away against the hillside. They spread out and rode at a trot until they were near the dugout, and then Mark and Joe swerved aside and rode up to the hill while Brian swung down from his mount and stood behind a tree facing the dugout. Brian called out, "Red Carson! Come out of there with your hands held high!" There was no answer, but after a moment a gun barrel was poked through the single opening that served as a window for the dugout. Brian raised his rifle and triggered two fast shots, one of which hit the gun barrel, and a yell sounded from inside the dugout. "Hold your horses," a voice cried out. "I'm coming out!"

A man who was built like a bear, with a head of shaggy red hair, slowly walked out of the dugout with his hands held high. "Anyone else in there?" Brian called out. The man shook his head and said, "No, I'm alone. I don't know you, so what's this all about?" Brian ignored him and shouted out loud, "Mark, Joe, shoot through the entrance and the window. Fill that room full of lead!" Joe had been gathering small dried branches from a fallen pine tree, and he had tied them together to make three bundles. He now set fire to two of them and threw the third across to Mark, who also set it on fire. Then they advanced cautiously, and while Mark lobbed the burning bundle through the open door, Joe did the same through the window, being careful to stand against the wall. Then Joe drew his six-gun and triggered two shots through the window. There was a yell from inside and a voice cried out, "Hold it! We're coming out!" Two more men came out with their hands in the air. "Anyone else inside?" Brian called out. The men shook their heads, and Brian said, "Joe, light some more torches and throw them inside!" Joe began tying dead branches together and Mark also did the same. Then they lit them and threw them in through the entrance and the window. Soon there was a roaring fire inside the dugout and the place filled with smoke. Suddenly there was a yell from inside, "Don't shoot!" A man came stumbling out the door, coughing continuously from all the smoke, and he fell to his knees when he was a safe distance away from the fire. Brian told the three men, "Drop flat to the ground and keep your hands behind your backs." The men complied, and while Joe and Mark went to tie them up, Brian walked over to the man who was still coughing badly, and he jerked the gun from the man's holster. Then he pushed the man face downwards on the ground and proceeded to tie his hands behind his back. Joe went into the trees and came back with four horses, and he and Mark picked up the tied men and draped them over the saddles. As they were lifting up the huge red-haired man, Mark remarked, "Ole Red here is really a bear!" But Brian told him, "That ain't Red Carson, this one is." He pulled up the man who was still coughing a bit, and Mark and Joe stared at him. The man was slightly built, with narrow shoulders, and he had a full head of pale blond hair that was almost white. Mark said, "*That's* Red Carson!?" Brian pointed to the man's holster and showed Mark the pistol he had taken from it. The holster and the butt of the pistol were smooth and well worn, and while the man himself looked dirty and disheveled, the gun and holster looked well cared for. "Guess his strength lay in his speed on the draw!" Brian remarked. Catching the man by his neck and belt, he heaved him across the saddle. After tying the men to the horses, they rode back to town.

They locked up the four men and then went to the Silverline Saloon. "So how many more men does Red Carson have?" Brian asked Flint. "Well, let's see now," Flint said. "You took out Seth Walker and Dillon, and you've got those three men plus Hook and his two friends in the lockup. Now you've brought in Carson with three more of his crew, so that adds up to... twelve!" He thought for a moment and then said, "I'd say about eight or ten more, but I don't know where they stay when they're not in town." Brian said, "I'm sure ole Red will know." Flint asked him, "What makes you think that he's going to tell you anything?" But Brian just shrugged and said, "Oh, I think he'll tell me whatever I want to know." They went back to the Marshal's office and Brian opened the lockup and said, "Red, come out here!" Red Carson came out cautiously, and Brian kicked a chair toward him and said, "Sit down! You're going to answer some questions I have." Red sat down and glared at Brian. "You may have questions," he spat. "Don't mean I'm going to answer!" Brian sighed and said, "Tie him up, Mark!"

Mark tied Red's hands behind the chair and tied a rope around his chest, holding him to the chair. He then tied his legs to the legs of the chair and stood up. "There you go," he told Brian. "Trussed like a Thanksgiving turkey! You going to do that Apache thing?" Joe asked, "What Apache thing?" Brian told him, "I spent a long winter one time in an Apache camp, and they showed me some of the things they do to test a man's courage." He paused for a moment in thought and then said, "I figure they had one test that worked the best." Joe asked him,

"What test was that?" Brian said, "They told me that the toes were the most sensitive part of the human body, so they would set fire to a man's toes. I never saw a man who lasted more than a minute before he was squealing like a stuck pig!" He bent down and began pulling off Carson's boots, while Carson's eyes opened wider and wider. "Hey!" Carson shouted. "You're a white man! You can't do such things!" Mark laughed and told Joe, "Times like this, I swear ole Brian here is more Apache than white. There was this one time he did this to a claim jumper in Arizona. That man was tough and he laughed at Brian and told him that he wasn't going to answer him."

"So what happened?" Joe asked him.

"Well," said Mark, "Brian set fire to his toes, and within a minute, he just couldn't answer fast enough; his words were tumbling all over each other! I put out the fire, and he gave us all the answers we needed." Joe looked at Carson speculatively and said, "How long do you figure Red here will hold out?"

Mark looked at Red Carson in an appraising fashion and said, "I don't think he's going to break the record!"

Brian had tied rags around Carson's toes, and now he told Mark, "Hold the chair so that he can't throw himself sideways or backwards." Mark went behind Red and held the chair while Brian took out a box of matches.

Red Carson shouted, "You're crazy! I ain't going to talk!"

Mark said sadly, "I sure hope you do talk, Red. Because if you don't, then the next trick he'll do is to set fire to your tongue!"

Brian struck a match and held it to the rags until they caught fire.

Red screamed, "Stop, stop! I'll answer your damn questions!"

Brian pulled off the rags, which were just starting to burn, and stomped on them to put out the tiny flame. "How many men do you have left?" he asked Red. "Where can I find them?"

Red's eyes were still popping out of their sockets, and he

shouted, "Two miles in a straight line from my dugout there's a building. It stands alone in a grove of trees. That's where most of my men stay! There should be five of them there right now."

Mark untied him and led him back to the lockup.

They were riding to the house when Joe asked Brian, "You really would have set fire to his toes and then his tongue?"

Brian laughed and told him, "That tongue part was Mark's imagination!" Turning serious, he said, "The trick is to make them believe that you will do what you say. Back in Arizona, we didn't have to do anything to that man. He believed that I would, so there was no need to do anything." After a moment, he added, "But I would do what I said if they didn't believe me!"

Joe looked uneasy, and Mark told him, "Pa always taught us that when dealing with vermin like this, nice ways don't work! They just love people who believe in good Christian ways, but show them the ways of the Apache, and they'll cave!"

Brian said, "Not all of them, but most men of this type are basically bullies, and a bully is most always a coward."

They reached the grove of trees and dismounted when they could see the house. The house was just a large log cabin, and it was built in a clearing about ten feet away from a small stream. They tied the horses to a tree and moved forward cautiously on foot. When they were about fifteen feet away, they stopped and surveyed the cabin and the land around it. There were five horses tied to a hitching rail in front of the cabin. The cabin itself had just the one door and one window on one side.

Brian told Mark, "Let's do that fire trick. You circle around and set fire to the back wall and then come back here."

Mark chuckled, "That always works! Pity though that we don't have any dynamite!"

Brian and Joe stood facing the door and window of the cabin with their rifles held ready. After about ten minutes, Mark approached them and said, "That there is real dry wood, and we should see some action pretty soon now." He moved back the way he came to keep the back of the cabin in his sights. Mark was right, because soon smoke started rising from the back of the cabin, and there was a yell from inside.

"The cabin's on fire!" a man shouted. "Bob, you and Shell take those buckets to the stream and put out the fire!"

Two men came running out of the cabin with buckets in their hands and raced to the stream at the back of the cabin. Three more men came out of the cabin, cursing, and Brian shouted out, "You men drop your guns and lie face down on the ground!" The men looked around wildly and then, drawing their guns, made a dash to get back inside the cabin. But before they could make it, Brian and Joe's rifles spoke, and the three men dropped to the ground. Mark fired two shots and brought down the two men who had gone to get the water.

Brian told Joe, "Tie them up first, and then we'll check their wounds."

He shouted out, "Mark, stay put until I get there!"

"I hear you!" Mark shouted back.

Joe tied the three men while Brian held his gun on them, and then they went over to Mark and Joe tied up the remaining two men; after which they put out the fire with water from the stream. All the men had been shot in their legs, which was where Brian, Mark, and Joe had aimed. They wanted to bring them down but not kill them, so they aimed for the legs. They tied up the wounds, and Brian asked one of them, "Red said there were eight of you here, so where's the other three?"

The man looked puzzled and said, "Red said that? He knows there are only five of us here. The rest are in town right now."

Brian had just been checking to see if Red Carson had told the truth, and now he said, "Tie them to their horses, and let's go back to town."

They put the wounded men in a dugout and deputized two miners to keep a watch on them. Back in the Marshal's office,

Brian held a discussion with Flint and the Wells Fargo agent, who was a rugged-looking individual named Dan Willoughby.

"I think we've got the entire Red Carson gang," Brian told them. "But now that we've got them, what do you plan on doing with them?"

Dan Willoughby shrugged and said, "Wells Fargo is responsible for the gold once it's deposited with us, but we don't really interfere in matters that concern the town. I figure the town will have to decide what to do with them."

Brian told him, "They can't hold them here forever, and even if they sent for a federal Marshal, that would take time. They could release them because Red Carson won't be able to work his claim-jumping scheme anymore in this town. So what do you think Red Carson would do once he's released?"

Dan frowned and asked him, "What are you saying?"

Brian told him, "I think that's obvious! If he can't run his claim-jumping scheme, then he's going to try to rob that gold. Now, there's two ways that he can do that. He can rob the gold before it's deposited with Wells Fargo, or he can rob it when Wells Fargo dispatches it from here."

Mark explained to Dan, "What Brian is saying is that this ain't just the town's problem, its Wells Fargo's as well. You let that gang go free, and you're putting your men in constant danger."

Dan Willoughby sighed and asked, "So what do you want me to do?"

Brian said, "Throw your weight behind the town's citizens because you know that Wells Fargo carries a lot of weight with the authorities. Hold a trial, find them guilty, and then Wells Fargo can transport them to the federal authorities. That way, the town is safe, and Wells Fargo gets rid of a real danger to their gold shipments."

Dan thought for a moment and then said, "I'll run it by my

boss, but I think you're right. So what will we do about a judge?"

Brian told him, "The town council will appoint you as a Justice of the Peace, and you can hold the trial. In an unsettled area like this, that would be perfectly legal."

Red Carson had been listening to the discussion, and now he shouted out from his cell, "I'll get free, and then I'm coming for all of you. Trust me on that!"

Brian walked up to the bars and told him, "I'll tell you what, Red. I think you figure yourself to be a real hard man with a gun. You're a scrawny-looking specimen, and except for that gun, I figure you've nothing much to shout about. You figure you're mighty fast on the draw, ain't that so? But I have my doubts even on that!"

Red glared at him and said, "I don't have to figure! You want to find out, you're going to have to face me."

Brian seemed to ponder that and then said, "You know what, Red? I think I really want to find out, but I also think that you're too yellow to face up to a man with a gun. I think that there's a big yellow stripe running all the way down your back!"

Red snarled, "You talk a lot! Face me, and we'll see who's yeller!"

Brian shrugged and said, "I'll tell you what, Red. You beat me, and you go free. No trial, no nothing…you just go free. How's that for a deal!" Red laughed and told him, "I'll take it, and I'll go free. Just give me my guns and face me! I've killed eleven men so far in gunfights, so you can make it twelve!"

Brian looked at him thoughtfully and then, opening the cell door, commented, "That would make a nice round figure."

They walked out of the Marshal's office, and in the street, Brian told Mark, "Give him his gun."

Mark handed Red his gun and gun belt, and while Red was buckling on the belt, the rest of them moved back to leave a clear space of fifteen feet between Brian and Red. Brian waited patiently while Red buckled on and then adjusted his belt and tied down his holster. With his hand hovering above his gun, he snarled at Brian, "Now you're going to make the…" He didn't complete what he was going to say because Brian simply palmed his gun and shot him twice. The first bullet took Red in the chest, and the second bullet ripped through his throat. Red fell dead with his gun still in his holster.

Flint was curious and asked Brian, "He said that you talk a lot, and you did back there in the office. What was that about?" But it was Mark who explained. "It's possible that Red's friends would have set him free when he was being transported to federal prison," Mark said. "That would mean that we would be looking over our shoulders for a long time to come. Brian was just egging him on to end this matter right here and right now. Red was sure of himself, and so he accepted the deal."

Joe said thoughtfully, "What Red didn't know was that Brian doesn't talk come shooting time, so I guess Red figured to have his say before drawing." He paused and then added wryly, "That's a bad mistake to make when facing a Bailey!"

Brian told Dan, "Red was the leader, and without him, the rest of the gang won't be a problem. I figure you can now transport them without too much trouble."

The trial was held, and a jury of miners and the town residents found the gang guilty and sentenced them to hang. Dan Willoughby arranged for them to be transported to a federal prison, and the town of Silver City heaved a sigh of relief.

CHAPTER 14
SETTLING DOWN

BRIAN, MARK, AND JOE RODE TO CHET ALLEN'S CLAIM, and as they dismounted, Sue Allen came running out from behind a pile of rubble and went straight to Brian. "A miner told us that you cleaned up the Red Carson gang," Sue told him. "He also said that you shot it out with Red Carson." She stared at him and then said, "You must be real fast on the draw because I've seen Carson draw against two men in town!" Brian just shrugged and said, "He talked too much. Now let's get this gold out for you and your Grandpa!" They worked hard, and by the end of two weeks they had exhausted the seam of gold. They sacked up the gold and rode to town to deposit it with Wells Fargo.

During the two weeks spent mining the gold, Sue and Brian had talked a lot after work each night and Brian realized that he was in love with her. On the last day, when they were sacking up the gold and getting ready to ride to town, Brian was silent and pensive. Sue came up to him and said, "Why the sad face, Brian?" He shrugged and muttered, "I ain't sad! Why would I be sad!" She just stood there looking at him, and finally he said, "Well, I guess now that you've got the gold, you'll be riding home with Chet." She touched his arm and said, "I don't have a home, Brian, but I will have one soon." Brian asked her, "So where are you planning on settling down, and can I come and visit?" Sue suddenly laughed, "You were telling me about that valley near the Animas, so that's where we'll be building our home!" For a moment Brian just stared at her, and then what she had said sunk in and he shouted, "You're saying you'll marry me?" Mark, Joe, and Chet had been watching the two of them, and now Mark said, "You better marry her, Brian, or ole Chet here will take out his shotgun!" Chet laughed and said, "No need for that. You got you a choice, son, you either marry her or you'll have to draw against her; and I wouldn't bet on your chances if you drew on her!" Sue cried out, "Grandpa! I told you before not to try and scare him away!" Chet smiled and said gently, "And I told you, child, this man just don't scare! I'm happy that you've found yourself a good man, and once we see a preacher to marry the two of you, I guess I'll be on my way." Brian protested, "No, Chet, you're coming with us, and you'll stay with us!" Chet sighed and asked him, "You sure about that, Brian?" Brian nodded, and Chet said, "That would make me very happy indeed, and the gold will be Susan's wedding gift." Sue told Brian, "Grandpa and I talked it over, and with the stake you have, together with this gold, we figure we have enough to start that ranch you were talking about." Brian said, "The ranch will be for us and for Mark and his wife, so we are talking about building two ranch houses." Sue turned to Mark, "Oh! I didn't know you were married, Mark!" Brian laughed and told her, "He's not married, not yet. But he will be as soon as he gets back to Red Butte in New Mexico!"

After depositing the gold with Wells Fargo, they decided that all of them would ride to New Mexico, where they would have a double wedding. Dewey Long rode into town, and he and Joe decided to ride with the Baileys to New Mexico. Joe told the brothers, "I figure it's my duty to watch your backs, seeing as how you boys are all starry-eyed now!" They all laughed, and then Joe told Brian, "Dewey and I thought that with our share of the gold, we could maybe start ranching near you in that valley." He paused and then added, "If that's okay with you." Brian gripped his shoulder and told him, "It would be an honor to have you as a neighbor. In fact, Bill Riley told me that once a town starts up, he's going to come in and open a saloon." Mark said, "That there's a wild and lonely land, and I for one am glad that two fighters like you and Dewey will be there with us. Now let's go celebrate the future!"

ABOUT THE AUTHOR

Terence Newnes was born in south India. He dropped out of college and during the 70s and 80s he worked in fabrication, machine shops, and tool rooms. He then worked a short stint in Ethiopia. At the age of 43 he became a certified medical transcriptionist and worked in Toledo, Ohio as a medical transcriptionist, editor, and finally shift team lead. He started his own business of call center and data entry in 2006. During the pandemic and lockdown he lost his business and went broke, but he never lost hope. He started writing, which was a childhood dream, and he has never stopped.

To learn more about Terence Newnes and discover more Next Chapter authors, visit our website at www.nextchapter.pub.

The Bailey Brothers
ISBN: 978-4-82419-847-1

Published by
Next Chapter
2-5-6 SANNO
SANNO BRIDGE
143-0023 Ota-Ku, Tokyo
+818035793528

3rd October 2024

This book is dedicated to my children:
May you always be close.